MURDER

on the

MOTHER ROAD

Cover Design by Karen Philips
Formatting by Debora Lewis arenapublishing.org

ISBN 978-0-9972349-1-6

MURDER
on the
MOTHER ROAD

A Bobby Navarro Mystery

GLENN NILSON

This book is dedicated to Reseda

ACKNOWLEDGMENTS

One of the priceless things a writer hopes to find is good feedback. It isn't always easy to hear, or apply to the work in progress, but, without that feedback, the final work would not be nearly as good. I am grateful to my readers, Lesley Diehl and Jan Day, for their time, effort and writing acumen and their willingness to help me improve my rough drafts to reach a final manuscript that is far better than I could have achieved on my own.

CHAPTER ONE

I'M NOT A cop, not even a detective, so I have no reason to get involved in a murder investigation. Unless the police think I did it. Or I'm asked to do a favor by a very pretty police officer. Or, I can't get the image of a young girl's corpse out of my head.

It was hot crossing the Mojave from Needles, triple digit hot. On my Harley, it had felt even worse, but now, up on the plateau in Arizona, the heat was pretty much bearable. Grasses on the rangeland spread out to form green meadows and forests of ponderosa pine offered scented shade to man and beast alike. Ahead lay Williams, gateway to the Grand Canyon. At least that's what the sign boasted. The south rim of the Canyon was still eighty miles off to the north, but Williams offered a good place to get off the road for the night. I had a reservation at a motel there, and knew of a good steakhouse.

I took the Williams exit off Interstate-Forty and eased my way back along the access road to the main strip, actually part of old Route 66. The straight pipes on my bike rumbled contentedly as I idled along the one-way street taking everything in. Tourists were out and about, checking the shops along the thoroughfare, buying ice cream or a cool drink, or looking for something to do until dinnertime. I looked forward to grabbing a shower, washing off the sweat and road grime, and then having a cold beer.

Of course, things always happen at a bad time. I heard a metallic whump and tinkle of broken glass. Someone up ahead had just banged into the car in front of them as they maneuvered to park, or were doing a bad job of getting out of their parking place. I slowed to a crawl with a funny feeling about what was going to happen next. Sure enough, the driver backed up a little, cut the wheel and started to drive off. I pulled alongside and yelled at him.

"You hit that car!"

The driver looked at me through the open window on the passenger side. It was an expensive car, and he was dressed well, from what I could see.

"That wasn't me," he said.

"I saw you do it!"

He shrugged and made a face. "That's why people have insurance." He gunned the engine and drove off.

I hate it when people bang into someone and don't take responsibility, so I swung my bike into the place he'd left vacant and dropped the kickstand. I didn't have much to write on, but I found a receipt from lunch jammed down inside my jeans pocket and a pen inside a leather pouch on the side of my pack. I did the best I could to write down the license plate and a description of the offending car. When I finished, I walked to the front, thinking I'd stick the note under the windshield wiper. Unfortunately, something was smelling pretty ripe. I glanced around to see if a dead animal was close by. I didn't see anything, so I put the note under the wiper blade. Probably wouldn't do much good, but it made me feel better to be doing *something*. As I turned back toward my bike, an old man appeared in the doorway of the shop next to me and looked out from the half-concealing shadows.

"Did you see that?" I said.

He looked at me, his face without expression. "See what?"

"Somebody hit this car and drove off... just now."

He shrugged. "Didn't see nothing. Didn't hear nothing."

Why are people so afraid to get involved? I mean, this was no big deal, but his deep-set eyes suggested he meant to say no more on the matter—almost defied me to try to make him.

The foul, heavy odor continued to fill the area. I told myself an injured animal must have crawled off to die in the weed-grown space between the buildings. Insects droned ominously, and flies continued to buzz around my head. There was no air moving. I felt sweat trickle down my spine. My feet had grown clammy and my boots were hot and heavy.

I straddled my bike and sat down, but then just remained there a couple of minutes. Another car drove by. I stared at the back end of the Buick that had been bumped. The tail light was busted, and the fender had been crunched in a bit. A paper, temporary license was taped to the inside of the rear window, indicating a recent purchase. A small medallion was fastened to the left side of the trunk lid advertised Ben's Autos. Along the rear seal for the trunk lid a small bit of cloth hung limp, and out of place. Not a rag, more like a piece of garment, a shirt, or something. I turned to see if the old guy was still watching from the doorway. He ducked back into the shadows, and vanished.

Resigned to checking this thing out on my own, I stood up. I had to know—one way or the other. The piece of cloth had probably caught in the locking mechanism when the trunk was closed, keeping the lid from locking securely. It stood slightly ajar. I looked around to see if anyone else was coming along. The owner maybe. Someone else who saw the fender-bender. Someone who smelled what I smelled. No one.

I slipped my fingertips under the trunk lid and tested it. With a creaky grown of hinges, the lid came up and I jerked backward, nearly falling in my reaction to pull away from the trunk—and what was in it. I'd seen dead bodies before—too many of them. I'll never forget this one though. Never forget her face. She was young. Maybe even pretty, but it was hard to say; the heat and the business of decomposition had bloated her face and body—but not the milky, open-eyed stare of her eyes.

She was naked, her lips cracked and puffy, and her mouth open—maybe from a final attempt to scream—or ask for mercy. Dried blood and mucous streaked her nose and the area around her mouth. Bruises suggested somebody had gripped her arms—with a lot of force. More bruises and a dark line on her neck added information to the picture I was getting—one that would haunt me for a long time. Jumping back when the trunk lid popped open wouldn't block out that image, and I couldn't reverse time and make it not happen. I'd found her body, and couldn't avoid having to take the next step.

Chapter Two

PART OF ME wanted to turn away and climb back onto my motorcycle, but it was only a small, inward part, a self-protective, feeling part. The rest of me did what I was supposed to do. Like I said, I've been through situations where someone was killed, not that I think you ever get used to that sort of thing. I mean, you get so you have a way of handling it so you don't see the dead *person,* just the dead body. I knew I shouldn't think about the girl who had been alive not so very long ago. But, I was having trouble blocking those thoughts out.

I knew I had to report this to the police. That was the next step. I pulled my cell phone out of my pocket. When I got the police dispatcher on the phone, my voice was steady. Technically, calling the police was all I had to do. Maybe that was all I should have done. That, and maybe try to keep others back, people who seemed to materialize out of the sidewalk to gawk and be horrified. I sat down on my bike to wait for the police. The dispatcher had told me to stay put. He even tried to keep me talking to make sure I did. I hung up on him. Not so I could drive off, but because I couldn't stand to chitchat just then, and I didn't give a damn what he wanted.

The police arrived in a tsunami of screaming sirens and howling engines, while the bystanders went from frantic cries of "Omigod, what *is* that—is that a *body* inside that car?" to the kind of hush that eventually always seems to settle over a scene with a dead body in it. I didn't bother to look around to count how many people had gathered. Instead, I stared toward the Buick with the trunk lid raised like the maw of some giant beast. An officer came up and stood next the car trunk.

"You the one who called this in?" he asked, pointing his outstretched hand back in my direction while taking in the girl's body at the same time.

I nodded slowly to acknowledge what my role had been. He turned in time to catch my movement.

"Just stay put 'til I've had a chance to talk with you," he said. Then he turned his attention to securing the scene.

I stayed where I was, while he and other officers pushed the onlookers back and put up ribbons of crime scene tape to construct a boundary. One of the police told me to step off the bike and go behind the tape.

"He stays right where he is," the first one said. "I need to talk to him yet." Then he pulled an emergency blanket from the trunk of his cruiser and spread it over the girl's body, still inside the trunk. When he did, he glanced at the gawkers, frowned and repeated his orders to keep back and not interfere with anything. The crowd of onlookers was getting larger. He spoke in a firm, loud voice. "If you know anything about this, we'll need to talk with you. Otherwise, there isn't anything here for you to do. Go on about your own business. There's nothing you can do to help."

Another car roared up the street and stopped, blue lights flashing from a dashboard mount. A man wearing dark slacks, and a white dress shirt with a necktie with the knot pulled loose, got out, glanced around to take in the scene, then ducked under the tape and approached the other officers. The police obviously knew him, and quietly filled him in on all that had taken place.

The officer in plain clothes looked toward me. "Get some information on him," he said. Then he turned his attention to the girl's body.

It didn't take as long as I had been afraid it might for the officers to take down my name, how I found the body, and so forth. When they finished, the plain-clothes guy came over and had me repeat everything to him. Then he introduced himself, without shaking hands.

"I'm Detective Sergeant Alvarez," he said. "Are you planning to stay with us for a few nights?"

I shrugged. "When I pulled off the highway, I just thought I'd take in the Canyon. I can't say that has much appeal right now, though."

"It would help if you keep yourself available for little while. You might remember something else. Or some questions might come up and I'll need to get in touch with you. I'd appreciate it if you didn't leave right away. If you decide you want to leave, check in with me first."

I nodded.

He looked at me carefully, then told me I was free to go, but reminded me again not to leave town.

I hit the starter, straightened the bike and popped up the kickstand, then eased my way toward the bystanders lining the crime scene tape. One of the uniformed cops raised the tape above his head to let me pass. I nodded and gave the engine more gas to head up the street. Numbly, I shifted through a couple of gears and looked for the sign for my motel.

The fellow at the registration desk inside the motel was dark-skinned, quiet, efficient, and very curious about what was going on down the street. "You came that way, didn't you? You must have seen what was going on."

I nodded, and mumbled something, keeping my eyes focused on the registration form I was trying to fill out. My fingers felt like I'd forgotten how to write with a ballpoint pen. "Someone got killed," I said. "You'll probably be able to catch it on the news tonight."

He looked at me, alert, eyes wide, head drawn back into perfect alignment with his spine. "Do you mean an accident? An automobile accident, perhaps?"

I shook my head. "More like someone was murdered. A body was left in a car, parked just down the street. Abandoned, I assume."

"Oh, my god, this is horrible! You were there? You saw the body?"

"Not something I want to talk about."

"No, of course not. I understand completely."

He looked in the direction where it all happened. "Many people find such things curious, though. I don't mean you are one of these people. Not like those who stand around as though they are spectators at some event."

"I may have to stay an extra day, or so," I said. "Police orders."

"Yes, of course. By all means. We do have reservations, however. I cannot guarantee the same room for you. Many people this time of year... tourists coming to see the Grand Canyon."

I shrugged. "Can't be helped."

"I'll do what I can, but you will let me know very soon?"

"Soon as I know, you'll know."

"Very good, then." He handed me back my credit card and the key to my room.

"I put you on the ground floor, Mr. Navarro. Down at the end of the building. I noticed you have a motorbike, and understand from other guests we have had, people with motorbikes like to be near them. That way, no one is likely to bother their motorbike."

"Thanks," I said. "I appreciate it."

"So... was there anything else you can tell me about what happened? Other guests will surely be asking me for information."

I shook my head and turned toward the exit. "I suspect everything will be on the news," I said. I pushed the office door open and stepped out into the heat.

When you're on a motorcycle, you can't carry all that much, so you'd think it would be easy to unpack what you do have. The thing is, each night you have to decide how much you want to leave on your bike, and what you need to take inside. I have leather saddlebags, easily opened by any fool with enough larceny and attitude to go for it. I don't have those custom made duffle bags that fit inside your saddlebags, so I end up putting some things here, and some things there, all with a great plan to make access easy, but I usually have to dig through everything anyway whenever I get to where I'm stopping for the night. I grabbed what I figured I needed, and a couple of things I'd probably want, and carried the lot inside.

I dumped my gear on the bed, turned the air conditioner on max, and started to strip things off, thinking about that shower. I paused long enough to dig a small bottle of bourbon out of my gear and turn the TV on to have some background noise. I picked up the bottle, worked the cap off and took a heavy swallow. My throat tightened as it burned its way down to my stomach. I took another, then put the cap back on and tossed the bottle onto the bed. As the bourbon sent a warm flush through my body, I finished stripping off my clothes, went into the bathroom and started the shower.

Water is scarce in Arizona. I knew that, even if most tourists don't, or choose to ignore the need to conserve. Usually, I take care to make any shower a quick one. This time, I didn't. Too much I needed to wash away. The reason I was on this trip was to do a favor for an old friend. I'm a blaster. He had asked me to blow up the entrances to some abandoned mines so no one could make the mistake of entering one of the rundown shafts and getting hurt. Actually, a couple of kids did just that while I was en route. One was killed. I met the family and the kid who survived. I had been having trouble dealing with the death of the kid who hadn't. Now, there was this girl's body.

I shut my eyes and turned my face into the shower. It was a relief just to stand there a while. However, all things come to an end, they say, and I finally turned off the water and grabbed a towel. The air conditioner was working pretty well, so when I stepped back into the room I felt a delicious, prickly chill as the cool air hit my damp skin. I rubbed my head with the towel to dry my hair. It's long and heavy. I guess I get that from my mother's side of the family, Apache. My father's Mexican. When I had my hair as dry as I was going to get it, I ran the towel down my back again and threw some clothes on. I was thinking I might be ready to face the evening when a heavy fist pounded on the door.

"Police! Open the door!"

DETECTIVE ALVAREZ STOOD facing me from the other side of the metal table in an interview room at the police station. A tape recorder lay on the tabletop, a pen and a blank notepad beside it. A uniformed police officer was standing sentry next to the door. I couldn't believe what I was seeing, I was pretty sure I recognized her.

The name badge said she was Officer Lucinda Diaz. I thought I knew her as Lucinda Hernandez. We went to high school together, although she was younger and two classes behind me. I can't say I would remember many of her classmates, but she had been a cheerleader, and the cutest of the bunch. I couldn't tell if she had recognized me yet, and wasn't sure she would want to, under the circumstances.

I decided not to make a point of it, and shifted my gaze to look around the room. There wasn't much furniture in it. Not much room, for that matter. Nothing on the walls except for what I took to be a small, two-way mirror. There was a sound of machinery rumbling through a ventilator opening in the ceiling. The air oozing through the small vent barely made it around the room, and smelled stale.

Alvarez's stubby neck glistened with sweat and damp blotches showed at his armpits. At least I'd had a chance to shower, and when I got dressed I had put on a clean Tee-shirt. I guess I should have felt lucky, but then, I wasn't here under the best of circumstances.

I glanced at Lucinda again. She looked composed, still pretty, but in a police officer sort of way, and professional—not friendly. Her duty belt seemed too large, which served to emphasize her slimness. She always had been slim. She had a little lipstick on, but no other makeup that I could tell. Her hair was done up in some sort of bun at the back of her head.

Alvarez interrupted my train of thought.

"Now, Mr. Navar... Or Robert.... Would you mind if I call you Robert?"

"Fine with me. Call me whatever... Most people call me Bobby."

I wanted to turn and see if hearing the name registered with Lucinda. I fought down the impulse.

Alvarez grinned and nodded his head as though happy with the progress he was making. "That's great, then. 'Robert' it is. So, Robert, why don't you tell us more about what happened today."

"What do you mean?"

"About the girl. Why don't you tell us more about what happened with the girl?"

I had a very bad feeling about the way he had phrased that.

"I already told you all I know," I said. "I stopped on my way into town because somebody hit the back of the car it turned out she was in. I stuck a note under one of the windshield wipers to let the owner know what happened."

Alvarez sat without saying anything. He could afford to wait. I was the one who wanted to get this wrapped-up.

"There was a piece of material keeping the trunk lid from locking all the way. I saw it hanging out" I said.

"Did that bother you?"

"What?"

"That the trunk lid hadn't locked down tight?"

"What do you mean, 'bother me'?"

Alvarez gave me a sympathetic smile. "Bothered you as in—unfinished business."

I thought about his question. Earlier, I had been afraid his suggestion, "Let's go down to the station where we can handle this more comfortably," had been a bad sign. Now, it was obvious he thought I killed her.

"I didn't have anything to do with it."

"With what?"

"Killing the girl. I didn't do it."

"I'm not saying you did, Robert. But, we know you were involved in it. Now we need you to tell us *how* you were involved."

"I didn't have anything to do with it."

"You brought the car downtown and parked it there on the street. You need to tell us what else happened."

"I just got in town. On my motorcycle. How am I supposed to have driven that car there?

Alvarez shook his head. "That's not how we heard it."

"This is crazy."

I shook my head. "Think about it. Why would I call you to report the body, if I had dropped the car off to dispose of it?"

"Good question, Robert. Why did you?"

"I didn't. I'm not the one who parked it there. I'm not the one who put the body in the damn trunk, and I'm not the one who killed that girl!"

Alvarez stared at me without expression. I could feel the pulse pounding in the veins of my neck. I sensed Lucinda looking at me from behind. At that point, I hoped she hadn't recognized me. Then my mind shifted gears, and I thought about his claim of having a witness. The old geezer in the doorway! The one who acted like he was half afraid of me and would barely speak.

"The old fart with all the whiskers?" I said. "He the one claiming I dumped the car?"

Alvarez smiled again, this time suggesting some small degree of satisfaction. "Who our witness is, isn't important to you right now, Robert. We have someone who says you parked the car where we found it."

I slumped back in the chair, brought my hands together and rested them on the tabletop. "Then you need to ask around and find some more witnesses. I stayed in Needles last night. I can prove it. I have a receipt for the motel, if not, I can get one; I paid with a credit card. This morning, I headed here. I stopped on the way and bought gas and some snacks. I paid with a credit card."

Alvarez nodded and wrote in a little notebook he pulled out of his pocket. "That's good, Robert. We'll check all that... we'll need to see those receipts."

Then I remembered I had written the note on one of them, the note I stuck on the windshield. Take a deep breath. Try to sound cooperative. Don't panic, just tell them what happened. Alvarez spoke up again.

16

"Well, that's another problem we have, Robert. We didn't see any note under the windshield wiper. Which one did you leave it under?"

I told him the one on the passenger side.

He shook his head. "We didn't see anything." He glanced toward Lucinda as though looking for confirmation. I didn't turn to see if she gave it.

"By the way," Alvarez said, "leaving the car right there on the main street of town—now that took real balls on your part. I have to hand it to you. Was that your idea, or did someone else come up with that one?"

I shook my head. "I didn't park the car; I was never in it. I'm not the one who killed her."

By that time, Alvarez wasn't the only one with drenched armpits, I was sweating too, and it wasn't due to the lack of ventilation. I watched him unfold his arms, pick up his pen and start tapping it on the notepad. "We're not saying you killed her, Robert. But you got yourself involved. It's time for you to man up and give us your side."

I stared at the tape recorder, hypnotized by the steady rhythm of the cassette wheels engraving each thing I said into something that might come back to cause trouble later.

CHAPTER FOUR

WHEN THE POLICE finally let me go, Lucinda was detailed to give me a ride back to the motel. I couldn't tell if she had recognized me yet. I kind of hoped not, given Alvarez's suspicions. My head ached and felt swollen. I couldn't seem to fill my lungs in one breath.

"You doing okay?" Lucinda asked.

It sounded more out of professional caution, or courtesy, rather than caring whether I was okay, or reflecting any sense of having recognized me.

"Considering the interrogation I just went through, I guess I'm okay."

She said it hadn't really been an interrogation, just an interview. "We need to find out what happened. Actually, we appreciate your being willing to come in and help us."

I shook my head. I couldn't accept the part about being appreciative.

She kept talking. "I can understand it might not have felt that way to you. But, we pretty much have to check out everyone, their accounts of everything, where they were, when—all that."

"Good thing I had that motel receipt, at least."

She settled into her seat a little. "Certainly helps. Your credit card company should be able to link us to your other receipts, or the gas station you used it at can provide a duplicate. It'll just take a little time, that's all."

Then she changed the subject. "So, you're here on vacation?"

Her comment sounded like a conversational opener, and felt totally out of place.

"You don't remember me, do you?" I said.

I thought my voice sounded disconnected. I had decided earlier I wouldn't tell her we knew each other, but the question just fell out of my mouth.

She hesitated, then spoke in a guarded tone. "I wasn't sure if you'd want me to recognize you. Sometimes people feel awkward...."

I nodded. I didn't know if she saw me in the rear-view. "I can appreciate that," I said.

"But, since you brought it up, of course I remember you, Bobby. We went to high school together."

I could see her take a good look at me in her rear-view mirror.

"This happen very often?" I asked.

"You mean running into someone I used to know?"

"Right."

"Well, I've never run into anyone from high school before. I mean, since I got married and moved away."

So, she was married. Well, that shouldn't come as a surprise.

We were at my motel. I told her my room was at the end, where the Harley was parked. She stopped the cruiser next to my bike.

"It was nice seeing you," she said.

"Would have been better under other circumstances," I said.

She made an awkward sounding chuckle. "I'm sorry about my reaction. I mean, I do remember you, of course I do. I just... had this sudden, horrible realization I might have to deal with someone I knew from way back—or, to be more honest, someone I used to hope would ask me out. I know everything will be fine when we check those credit card receipts, though. It was just a momentary reaction, that's all."

I was smiling. Hell, I was grinning from ear-to-ear. "I was having a similar reaction," I said. "I was embarrassed because you were seeing me in the worst possible way."

I saw her glance at me in the mirror, and I locked onto the sparkle of interest her eyes, then watched in helpless disappointment as the mask of her professional side pushed all that aside.

"Well, try to enjoy what you can of the rest of your stay," she said.

I told her I would.

"There's going to be a Rendezvous this weekend, if you're into that sort of thing."

"What's a Rendezvous?"

"Bunch of guys dress up like they think mountain men did in the old days, camp out and talk guns. Stuff like that."

"You ever go yourself?"

"I have. There's one every year. You should try it."

"I might."

She let a tiny hint of a nice smile slip into place on her mirror image. "Again, it was nice to run into you."

"Yeah, you too," I said.

I got out and watched her back around and drive out of the parking lot, thinking of the last time I remembered seeing her, at the Senior Ball. She was someone else's date. I danced with her once, though. It was a slow dance. I could almost remember how she had felt in my arms. Funny how much can change in a few years. Now, I wondered if I'd see her again.

CHAPTER FIVE

EARLY NEXT MORNING, the restaurant down the street was busy serving a mix of locals grabbing something before going to work and tourists up early and eager to get a start on whatever their day's plans might be. A counter ran the length of the room, like an "L" flipped over, with the short leg near the entrance and the long leg ending at a wall faced with stone. Pictures of famous figures from the fifties, Marilyn Monroe, James Dean and others, hung above the counter. Luckily, there was an empty seat near the front. I took it, and ordered an omelet with green chili, refried beans and a cup of black coffee.

"What kind of toast you want with that, Sweetie?" the waitress asked. She was blond, dressed in a white, uniform dress, and had a small, black apron tied around her waist with the pockets filled with her order book, soda straws, and whatever.

"Rye," I said.

"Coming right up. I'll bring you that coffee; need cream and sugar?"

"Just black."

She moved off, but turned her head to call back to me. "We're a little short-handed this morning. You'll have to be patient with us."

An intense looking guy, also sitting at the short leg of the counter, offered an explanation for her comment. "They took Ernesto last night."

I shrugged and turned toward him. He was younger than me, somewhere in his twenties. Maybe early twenties, but something about him made his age hard to guess. He was lanky, dressed in long, baggy cargo shorts and a worn tee shirt. His hands bore a stain of ground-in dirt and oil. He had a bad haircut that needed cutting again. An old scar tracked downward the length of his cheekbone, making his face look all the more sinister and hawk-like. I wondered how the scar came to be there.

"Who's Ernesto?" I said.

"He's one of the cooks."

"Okay, who took him, and why did they do that?"

"They think Ernesto killed that girl." He jerked his head toward the wall-mounted television at the end of the counter.

"Really?" I said.

The waitress was back with my coffee. It was like she had kept up with the whole conversation while she was gone. "I know it must look awful for him, but I just don't believe Ernesto could possibly be the guilty party. Ain't that right, Daryl?"

The guy at the counter nodded emphatically.

"Goddamned right," he said.

"Did they actually arrest him?" I asked. I was thinking about my own "interview" by the police.

The waitress nodded her head vigorously. "Late last night. It's been on the TV all morning." She raised her eyebrows. "It was Ernesto's car they found that poor little girl's body in."

I glanced at the television. I couldn't hear the announcer over the noise of the breakfast crowd. "Well, I'll be damned," I said.

"You knew we had a murder in town, didn't you?" the waitress said.

"I did."

The two went on to explain how Ernesto had been with the guy sitting near me, Daryl, working at one of the local churches. Ernesto had bought a used car. Daryl had suggested he take a break and go get some donuts, but when Ernesto went outside, his car was gone. He waited, and looked around, thinking somebody had taken it to play a joke. Finally, he ran out of time, and asked Daryl to give him a ride to the restaurant for his regular job. The police came and got Ernesto just before his shift ended. They also got to Daryl in the wee hours of the morning. At some point, they cut Daryl loose, but held on to Ernesto.

"Actually, the police thought I might have had something to do with it, too," I said. "We had a nice, long talk yesterday afternoon."

I gave them the short version of my own "interview". They listened like a pair of vultures hovering over fresh road kill. I finished my story with the police letting me go and Lucinda driving me back to the motel. I didn't tell them I knew her in high school.

"Well, they let you two go, but they sure haven't released poor Ernesto," the waitress said.

"Sons of bitches, it's just like last time—all over again."

"Oh, Daryl, don't get your tummy in a turmoil. Ernesto's going to be okay," she said.

A cook banged the bell on the pick-up counter several times and hollered, "Carrie!"

The waitress turned around. Orders had piled up beneath the heat lamps, and a couple of customers were giving her dirty looks. "Be right there, Darlin'. Doing the best we can here."

She gathered an armload of platters off the counter and carried them to a group of people sitting at a table at the other end of the room.

The guy next to me, "Daryl", asked if that was my motorcycle outside. I said it was.

"Good looking bike."

I thanked him.

"Where you from?" he asked.

"Upstate New York."

He frowned. "I don't like big cities."

I wondered if he had ever been to one.

"I don't either." When I say "New York" people always think I'm from the city. Upstate is different. It's all hills, farms and forest. Ever hear of the Adirondack Mountains, or the Catskills?"

He shook his head.

"Nice country. You'd probably like it."

He continued to stare at my bike. I had backed it into the parking place. Black, with black leather saddle bags and plenty of chrome studs, chrome sissy bar and ape-hanger handlebars. Daryl looked about to drool.

I cut off a bite of my omelet and sopped up some of the beans and chili sauce. Daryl lifted his fork, scraped it through the syrup on the bottom of his plate but then set it down again.

"Nobody in his right mind would kill somebody, lock them in the trunk of his own car, and then park it almost right outside where he works," Daryl said. "But, I guess that's what the police are claiming Ernesto did."

I thought about the old guy standing in the doorway, presumably telling the police he saw me park the damned car. "I guess they have to deal with whatever information comes their way," I said. "Maybe that doesn't always help finding out who really did it.'"

Daryl raised his head and looked into the distance. "Well, the police aren't going to find out who did it, now."

"Why not?"

He frowned at the cup in his hands. "Because they've got Ernesto."

"You two close? You and Ernesto?"

He shrugged. "Close enough."

"Maybe it'll still turn out okay."

He shook his head. "No fucking way. They've got Ernesto locked up, end of story."

Then his voice trailed off to a near whisper, like he was talking to himself. "Trouble is," he said. "I know who the hell did it."

He turned toward me, looking as startled by his comment as I felt hearing it. Then, just as quickly, he looked away.

"Did you just say you know who did it?"

His jaw tightened. He started digging in his pockets, pulled out some change along with a few crumpled bills and stood up.

"You should tell the police," I said.

He shook his head. "Wouldn't help none if I did. They already think I had something to do with it, me and Ernesto both. They're just looking for an excuse to throw me in jail now too. I'm not giving it to them."

He threw the money on the counter, turned and pushed open the big, glass door.

Maybe I should have got up and left, too. I didn't. I stayed for the coffee refill Carrie offered. I stayed because I had to think over the conversation I'd just had with Daryl. I stayed because I'm no good at avoiding trouble.

CHAPTER SIX

LATER, I DECIDED I needed something to get my mind off the murder—and Daryl. This part of the trip was supposed to be a vacation. At the motel, I asked the desk clerk about the Rendezvous Lucinda had mentioned.

It was a different clerk handling reception, a young woman. Her complexion was flawless, creamy with olive tones, eyes almond-shaped and large with a sense of humor sparkling down deep. She looked puzzled at my question, then her eyes widened and lit up in recognition of what I was asking about.

"Is that the thing where everyone dresses up, and they have guns and tents and such?"

"Sounds like it." I smiled.

"I have never been to one, but I think I know what you are talking about."

I followed her directions and found a grassy field with at least a couple hundred vehicles already there, parked in neat rows. A guy in an orange vest directing traffic waved me toward an area with some other motorcycles, close to the entrance. Being on a motorcycle often results in "preferred" parking. That can be handy. Well, it makes sense. You can get a number of bikes in the space one car would take up.

I shut the engine down, and climbed off, jammed my helmet on top of the sissy bar and strolled toward the action. A number of canvas tents had been set up along both sides of a flattened grass pathway. I took them to be the recreations of tents early explorers had used. They had steep roofs, some with cabin sides, and most had a fire ring in front. The sweet fragrance of cedar smoke drifted through the air, along with enticing smells of food being prepared. At one of the fires, a fellow with long, white hair and full beard sat stirring the contents of a kettle. He wore a coonskin hat, fringed leather shirt and had a large hunting knife tucked into his belt.

"Smells good, buddy. What are you cooking?"

"Some stew. I'll have it later for my supper."

He smiled and continued his explanation. "Mountain men—the brotherhood I belong to and consider to be my true forebears—ate a lot of dried meat. Venison, elk, whatever. This happens to be venison. I'm fixin' to let it simmer over the coals for a few hours. That way, it'll get tender. Then I'll add vegetables and have myself a proper mountain-man stew. Victuals fit for a king—the only wealth outside of fresh air and unspoiled views a true mountain man would likely have or want. That, and a few good friends."

I touched my fingers to my forehead in a parting salute. "Enjoy."

He raised his hand, palm facing me. "May the Great Spirit watch over you until our paths cross again."

I couldn't hold back a grin at the guy's performance, but hell, it was his show. I made my way toward a cluster of onlookers where some kind of contest seemed to be taking place, wondering if everyone else would act like the guy I had just met. When I got a little closer, I saw one of the last people I would have expected to run into there—Daryl, the guy from the diner. He wasn't dressed up all the way, but did have on a leather hat with a wide brim. He was looking toward a sawed-off round of a log. A playing card, the ace of spades, was fastened to the center of the round. Daryl and the other contestants stood in a line about twenty-five feet away. The first one drew back a Bowie-style hunting knife, measured the distance, and made his throw. The point stuck in the face of the log about five inches from the playing card. A cheer went up, so I guessed the crowd approved. I thought it was a miss.

Daryl was next. He drew his knife, raised it in front of him and focused on the playing card. When he was ready, he drew his arm back over his shoulder and swept it forward again, leaning into the release. The knife stuck into the card, very near the center spade. A cheer went up from the onlookers.

Daryl broke out in a satisfied grin, and he turned around to acknowledge the crowd. His expression registered surprise, then suspicion, as he spotted me standing among the rest. He went back to smiles just as quickly, turned and walked over to retrieve his knife. He pulled it from the face of the log and stuck it into the scabbard fastened to his belt, then looked my way with a dark expression on his face. He only held it for a second, before rejoining the line of competitors, with his back to me and the rest of the crowd.

I watched the rest of the competition. The winner was a man wearing a coonskin hat, fringed shirt, wool pants and high leather boots. His knife cut into the card about halfway between the edge and the center, beating out Daryl's throw by a half inch. I didn't wait around to say anything to Daryl after the contest, after all, I'd been trying to forget about him. There was still plenty of other stuff to look at. I moved off with the crowd and worked my way down the row of exhibits. I had my eyes on a tent that appeared to be offering barbeque and hamburgers. That's when I saw Lucinda.

She was out of uniform, and I almost didn't recognize her. She had let her hair down, literally, and it hung in dark waves around her face. Even prettier than I'd imagined it would look back at the police station. She wore lipstick and a little eye shadow. Close fitting jeans, hiking boots, and a plaid shirt completed her outfit. The tomboy effect added even more appeal. I've always gone for the outdoor type.

A young girl, around four or five years old, clung to her hand. Of course, Lucinda had mentioned being married when we were talking, but I didn't remember seeing a ring on her finger. The girl must be her daughter. So, was she single, or still married?

Lucinda looked up and saw me. I thought she looked uncomfortable. I tried telling myself she probably didn't want any crossover between her professional and private lives. Of course, what I really thought, was she didn't want anything to do with a murder suspect she went to high school with.

I nodded, trying to look casual and non-threatening.

She nodded back.

Then I realized I had continued to walk toward her. I stopped, and just stood there. She broke the awkward silence.

"Enjoying the activities?"

I tried a friendly grin. "It's been interesting, so far."

She smiled back, but like I had just pegged myself as a tourist. I needed to change the subject. "I see you brought a buddy along," I said.

I guess I sounded lame, but kids often get left out of adult conversations. Like they're not there. I don't like being one who does that.

"This is my daughter, Miguella." She looked down at the young girl. "This is Mr. Navarro—someone Mommy once knew, a long time ago."

Miguella gave me a big smile and stuck out her hand. I laughed, took it in mine and we shook hands.

"Nice to meet you," she said.

"I'm happy to meet you, too, Miguella. I'm here on vacation, and your mother was good enough to tell me about the Rendezvous. Are you having a good time?"

"Yes." She spoke in a very grownup voice. "I like it when Mommy has time to take me places."

I let her hand go and looked at Lucinda. The smile she held for her daughter brimmed with affection. It was a Kodak moment, seeing the two of them like that. Then Lucinda turned her head toward me again.

"I take it you don't have children of your own." It was her business face and her police officer voice.

"No, I don't have any children."

She straightened up, as though she wanted to move on and I was holding her back. "Nice running into you again."

I started to step aside, but had a second thought. "I don't mean to hold you up, but there was something I guess I should mention."

A look flashed across her face I took to be concern that I might be about to say something she wouldn't want her daughter to hear.

"It's probably nothing. But, this fellow at the diner where I ate breakfast this morning seemed to think he knows something about the business we talked about yesterday. His name was Daryl. I didn't get his last name. That's about all there is to it, but I thought I should say something."

I put it like that, quick and easy, no unpleasant details, and let it go. Just doing my civic duty. She studied my face a couple of seconds before replying.

"If there's more, you might want to come into the station and make out a statement."

"I'd be glad to."

Miguella pointed toward a booth with weavings and leather goods hanging from the support poles. She gave Lucinda's hand a little tug, impatient to be off.

"Can we go over there, Mommy?"

Lucinda glanced toward the exhibit, but didn't move. "Just a second, Sweetie."

"I told him, he should tell the police," I said. "But, he seemed to think you people wouldn't believe whatever he had to say."

She smiled in a way that seemed disconnected from our present discussion. "Did he talk much about it with you?"

"A little. He was sitting next to me at the counter." I shrugged. "I probably should have ignored him."

She gave her head a little shake. "Not necessarily. But, I'm surprised. The Daryl I know, is suspicious of just about everyone. I'm amazed he treated you any differently."

I waited to see where she would go with that.

"If you see him again, don't discourage him," she said. "And, if he does say more, I'd appreciate it if you'd give me a call."

"I'd be glad to."

She reached behind and pulled out her wallet, fished out a business card with her name and number at the police station on it, and gave it to me. I felt my pulse rate go up. Maybe I had been over-reacting. Maybe she didn't see me as a rapist/killer.

"Why don't you give me a call tomorrow, in any case? I'd like to talk about this some more."

"Sure, I'd be glad to." I felt like a kid trying to ask for a date for the first time. I hoped I didn't sound that way.

She edged past me without saying anything else, letting Miguella pull her toward the booth. I could smell her perfume as she brushed by, a very nice, flowery scent.

A few feet further, Miguella whirled half around and waved back at me.

"Bye." She cupped her fingers in a little wave.

"Bye," I said.

CHAPTER SEVEN

I CALLED LUCINDA first thing after breakfast next morning. She asked me to come into the station and said she'd wait for me. She must have said something to the officer sitting security, because he picked up a phone and let her know I was there without any question. Lucinda led me to a desk that evidently belonged to her, although it sat in a common area, and asked me to give her a full account of my conversation with Daryl.

"Daryl King," she said. "Interesting person."

I agreed.

"Obviously, I've had some dealings with him," she said. "Most all of us have at one time or another."

"Been in a lot trouble then?"

She frowned.

"Not that, exactly. He grew up with some anger issues. Mother died. Adoptive family members apparently had different feelings about his being there. He had some problems in the neighborhood, small things mostly. You know, "borrowing" another kid's bicycle, getting into fights, complaints at school. That sort of thing."

"Doesn't sound too unusual," I said.

"As he got older, things got more serious. In some ways, he was slow to develop. A woman in the neighborhood accused him of molesting her daughter, taking her underpants down. I know that sort of thing happens, but usually involves someone younger than he was."

"How far did it go?"

She shrugged. "From what I heard, he just pulled her pants down and checked her out."

I was curious to know just how old he had been at the time, but let her continue without interrupting her.

"After that, people got a little uneasy about him hanging around young girls. And that's something he did, hang around. He was a teenager by then, and seemed to have a thing for one girl in particular— Betsy Horvath."

I felt the skin on the back of my neck prickle at the thought of where this story might be leading.

Another officer walked past, pausing to glance at me and exchange hellos with Lucinda. She waited until we were alone again before continuing.

"Betsy was killed about two years ago. Raped and strangled. Her body was found in the forest, then later stolen from the morgue and never recovered. A young man was arrested for it, and he's still in prison. I've always thought maybe Daryl had a role in it too. We couldn't find anything on Daryl that would stick, nevertheless, I've always wondered what really happened."

"You think Daryl might have been in on Betsy's rape, murder, or both?" I said.

"With Sheri Norton's murder, and the comment Daryl made to you, I have to wonder about the possibility he might have been involved somehow in both."

"You guys are holding Ernesto for doing it. Are you saying, you think he's innocent?"

"No way, but I have a feeling we need to keep looking at Daryl, as well."

She had leaned forward and lowered her voice. "Back then, Daryl claimed he was Betsy's friend, but he could just as easily have been her stalker. Maybe the same can be said with Sheri. Ernesto's car puts him in the picture. But, he and Daryl might both have been involved. Trouble with Daryl is, he shuts down, starts showing his crazy side, and you can't get anything out of him. You end up spinning your wheels and trying to convince a public defender you aren't harassing a suspect. You're right, we have Ernesto locked up. Maybe he'll implicate Daryl somewhere down the road and give us something to go on. But, I'd like to get Daryl for Betsy's murder as well as this one. Assuming he had something to do with them."

She shot a glance around the office space, using just her eye movement. "I'd like to see if Daryl says anything to you that can shed light on both murders. I think you give us a good opportunity to see what he might have to say to someone he obviously isn't so suspicious of. I'd like to ask you to help us out."

I felt shocked when Lucinda said she wanted me to help out. One minute, they take me down to the station and interrogate me, and then next thing I know, she's asking for my help. I told her how stunned I was.

"As I explained to you," she said. "We have to check out everything. That's just doing our job."

"But now you trust me enough to ask for my help?"

She smiled. "I always liked you in high school. Looked up to you. I thought you were someone I could definitely count on then. I still think you are.

Besides, I believed you in here, when you gave your account of what happened."

"How about Detective Alvarez?" I asked.

"Again, he was just doing his job. I've already run this by him."

"How am I supposed to get close enough to Daryl to get him to open up to me; I don't know where he lives, works, or even hangs out?

"As to where he lives, I can give you an address," she said, grabbing a pen and writing something down on a piece of notepaper.

She handed me the paper. "I wouldn't show up there right away," she said. "Like I told you, he gets suspicious of people awfully easily. Try going back to the diner. He's probably a regular. Beyond that, play it by ear a little bit."

Lucinda escorted me to the station outer area, and I left with the heavy metallic sound of the security door closing behind me. I crossed the foyer to the main exit and stepped out into the bright sunlight. It felt good to be outside, even though the air conditioning inside had been pleasant enough. It felt especially good not to be a suspect. Of course, I suppose everyone's a suspect until a case is completely wrapped up, but it looked as though I wasn't a prime suspect, at least. I'd take that.

I walked to my bike, thinking over my conversation with Lucinda. She had said she looked up to me in high school. Was that sort of like, having a crush? I guessed not, although I felt good that she had liked me. The other night, I had doubts about her even recognizing me.

I had to admit, the fact that Daryl had talked with me once suggested he might say more. Maybe I could help out. Funny how things can change. I climbed onto the saddle and started the engine, telling myself the goal was to find out who was involved in Sheri's murder, and maybe Betsy's. If I could help do that, it would be good, right?

Right.

Of course, now I'd be working with Lucinda.

Right again.

And then, who knows?

CHAPTER EIGHT

I GAVE THE motel desk clerk a heads up that I was leaving, and started throwing my things together. Now that I had agreed to help Lucinda get more information from Daryl, I figured it made sense to move to cheaper surroundings. Living in motels can get pretty expensive, and my stay wasn't anything I could put on an expense invoice. Besides, I love camping.

On my way into town, there had been a campground advertised on one of those highway signs that tell you places available to eat, sleep, and buy gas. I looked it up in the phone book and called to see if they had any vacancies. There are a lot of people on the road, looking for a place to stay, especially near the Grand Canyon. Campgrounds often fill up fast. This time, I got lucky. They had a tent site open. I packed my bike, paid my bill and headed for the campground.

"Just fill this out, and we'll get you checked in," the woman behind the counter said.

I completed the registration form, paid for several nights, and drove to the tent site area.

Camping can be simple, or elaborate. I've watched people set up huge tents with multiple rooms, folding tables and chairs, hanging lanterns and gear bags, and that says nothing about the bicycles, swimsuits, water guns and other toys to keep the kids happy. I remember listening to a guy pumping up a queen size mattress for about forty-five minutes. I carry my sleeping bag, ground cloth and tent all rolled into one—no air mattress. Setting up is quick and easy. I had my tent up in about five minutes.

I knew I'd be wanting a fire later, so with my tent set up, I decided to scrounge up some wood for kindling. I'd seen a stack of dead branches on the side of the highway coming into town. If necessary, I'd go back and see what I could use. First, however, I thought I'd take a ride on some roads other than US-40. It was a beautiful day, and I was feeling good. Dry air, plenty of sunshine. Part of what I love about the West. I drove out of town, enjoying the rumble of exhaust pipes and the feel of the wind whipping against my face. When the Ponderosas gave out and the land opened up, there were still plenty of junipers growing on the range lands. I was hoping I might come across something cut down and allowed to dry out along the side of the highway. It happens sometimes. I wasn't disappointed. Some juniper had been put to the chainsaw and now lay in a graying tumble just off the pavement. I pulled over and dropped the kickstand.

There are rules about how large a knife a person is allowed to carry legally, and it isn't very big. Way smaller than the knives those guys at the rendezvous were throwing at their target. Mine was tucked into my pack and closer to rendezvous variety than to the legal size. I took it out of the pack and stepped over to the pile of dried wood, keeping an eye out for anything that might be lurking in the shade and safety of the branches. I don't mind rattlesnakes, as long are they're far enough away, but I don't want any close encounters.

The wood proved as dried out as I had hoped it would be, and I had no trouble snapping off a few branches and hacking them into pieces small enough for my purpose. They'd make good kindling. I tied a small armful on top of my pack with the tie-down straps I normally use to secure my tent and bedding role. Some clumps of sage were growing nearby, and on impulse I cut off a few small branches of this as well. I love the smell of sage, especially right after a rain. It occurred to me, I might want to take some with me when I went back to New York, once I was through here. In any case, I could enjoy the fragrance inside my tent.

When I got back to the campground, I discovered I had neighbors. Two women had begun setting up camp in the space next to mine while I was out gathering kindling. They had new-looking gear, still in boxes, in the back of what I guessed was their rental car. I watched them at work for a few seconds. One of them caught me looking and flashed a pretty smile and a quick, enthusiastic wave. I smiled back and said, "Hi."

They looked like they knew what they were doing, so I left them to it. Moving to the campground had two immediate effects. It took some of the pressure off wondering how long I could afford to put up in an expensive motel. It was nice, but not cheap, and I didn't want to run low on funds before I was ready to go back to work. The other effect was to give me a little more sense of commitment. I was no longer "hanging around" for a couple of days. I had a base camp, and I could stay there as long as I needed to. Well, I guess there was a third effect. I feel at home whenever I'm camping, and it was good to feel that way again.

I glanced at the two women to see how they were doing. It looked like they were getting set up quite well. The blond woman, the one who had waved, saw me and treated me with another big smile. She was gorgeous in a sophisticated sort of way. I couldn't explain how. Her companion was very attractive as well, dark hair, mid-calf-length pants, and a white top. I decided I should introduce myself.

When I started toward their campsite, they both straightened up. The blond brushed her hands together to wipe off any dust, and met me about where I imagined the boundary between our two sites would be.

"Hi," she said. "I'm pleased to meet you."

She stuck out her hand. "I am Jeanine Olsen."

Her face was bright and innocent. She spoke with an accent, which I found out was Norwegian. We talked for a while. I learned she and her companion were on a tour of the Southwest, taking in the Grand Canyon and what they could of old Route 66, before starting graduate studies at University of Southern California. The graduate school part made me half afraid to talk with them. I was afraid I'd say something wrong, or not know the meaning of a word they used, or not be able to understand what they were saying at all.

I can't stand awkward silences, and we were starting to generate one. Jeanine glanced at Anne a couple of times, like she needed to get back to work, and I couldn't think of anything to say. I decided the best thing, was to let them finish setting up their camp, so I told her to enjoy her stay, and walked to the office/store to check out what sort of supplies it carried.

Campground stores are pretty much the same over-all, but with little differences that make checking them out worthwhile. You never know. You can almost always pick up a can of ravioli, baked beans, or Spam. And you can get a loaf of bread or carton of eggs. Usually, you can buy ice cream. Of course, there are always souvenir Tee-shirts, shot glasses, mugs and post cards. I try to spot a supermarket near wherever I'm staying so I can improve my choices for meals. Sometimes I like to get elaborate in what I cook, and a fresh chicken leg, or steak, and some fresh veggies make camping life even better. At other times, it's just nice to have backup. Anyway, camp stores are fun to browse.

"Anything you need and you can't find, dearie, you just let me know," the woman running the office said. The tag she wore pinned to her blouse said her name was Agnes. She looked to be in her fifties, short gray hair, a little on the plump side, but not really overweight. Her smile seemed genuinely friendly, not customer-staged.

"I was just looking around."

"Here to see the Canyon?"

"Yeah," I said. "That, and doing a favor for an old friend."

She waited. I could tell she wanted me to say more, but I decided not get into all that.

"No big thing, really, but I'll be around for a little while."

"Well, you just make yourself comfortable dearie, and if there's anything we can do to make your stay better, you just holler."

I thanked her. A man opened a rear door and walked into the area behind the counter.

"This here's my husband, Russell," she said. "I'm always here, but if something comes up and I'm not, Russ can help you out."

I nodded.

Russell gave me an appraising look. He must have decided I was okay, because he stuck out his hand, taking a few steps toward me. We shook hands.

"You might want something other than a bare tent site, if you're going to be here for a spell," he said.

"Maybe, but I'm sure I can make out."

"I'll keep my eye open and let you know if anything better comes up. One of our little cabins would be just the thing. They're usually all booked up, but sometimes we get a cancellation."

"Okay, but I'm fine with a tent," I said.

I made my way toward the door, leaving the two of them grinning their welcome-to-the-campground smiles that seemed such a contradiction to my reason for staying there—helping look into the murders of two young women.

Chapter Nine

BACK AT THE campsite, Jeanine and Anne were piling the empty boxes their gear had come in next to their car and looking around for another place to put them. I decided to be helpful and offered to show them the dump bin at the other end of the campground. Jeanine and I carried the trash off while Anne stayed busy with other stuff.

"Have you camped here before?" Jeanine asked.

"Not here, but I've camped in a lot of other places."

"Actually, I have done a lot of camping too. Of course, most of my camping things had to be left at home. Anne and I plan to travel together to see America whenever we have the chance, so it made sense to get new equipment for our use here."

I nodded and told her I agreed. "The guy in the camp store thought you would be amateurs when he saw the boxes of new gear, but I guessed you were going about the tent setup too well for anyone new to the routine."

She laughed. "Oh, we both have experience camping. We have done much hiking in the mountains, and we carried backpacks when we did that. There, we sometimes stayed in shelters that were built for people to use, but not always."

Then Jeanine asked the question everyone does—what my visit was all about.

"It was supposed to be something of a vacation."

"But something happened to make it otherwise?"

"I found a body," I said.

She stared at me with saucer-wide eyes and a questioning look on her face. I told her the story of finding the body in the car trunk, and being questioned as a suspect.

"But you said they have arrested someone?"

I nodded. "But there may be someone else involved."

"Do you think the police suspect you of being that other person?"

"I don't think so. Not now, anyway."

I told her about my encounter with Daryl, and his claim that he knew who had murdered the girl. I also explained about Lucinda being a police officer, and a friend from high school, and told her about agreeing to help Lucinda by trying to learn more from Daryl.

Jeanine's eyebrows lifted. She tilted her head and appeared to think things over while we broke down the boxes and dumped them into the trash. When we finished and were headed back to our campsites she spoke up again.

"It seems very... how do you say it... heroic, that you are actually helping to find the person who murdered this young girl."

"I wouldn't call it heroic," I said. "I just can't get her face out of my mind. Opening that car trunk lid and seeing her body made the whole thing very personal, and unforgettable. Trying to get this guy to open up and tell me whatever he actually knows seems like the least I can do."

"Will you also be going around asking questions and investigating like on the police television shows?"

I laughed at her suggestion, and told her the police had already done their investigation, for the most part. "I'm really just following up and seeing if this guy says anything more. He probably won't, but it seems worth a shot."

"But he may be dangerous," she said. "He may have been involved, himself. So, what you are doing still sounds very heroic."

"Stubborn, is probably more like it," I said. But then I had a quick flashback to watching Daryl throw his Bowie knife, and the look in his eyes when he recognized me standing in the crowd.

Chapter Ten

LATER THAT AFTERNOON, Jeanine and Anne took off
for town, sporting big smiles and announcing they
were off to see the sights. I felt I needed a walk, and
decided to do some sightseeing of my own. Time to
give Williams a good once-over. Of course, I had also
decided to eat in town at the diner where I met Daryl.
I was hoping I'd run into him again.

Williams' downtown area is made up of two, back-
to-back one-way streets, a remainder of old Route 66.
I'm a people watcher, and I like to explore a town on
foot whenever I can. Williams has the kinds of shops
you'd expect to find in a town heavily dependent on
tourism, places selling curios, art galleries, and jewel-
ry stores selling Native American silver and turquoise. All-in-all, not bad for browsing. The buildings
had the feel of an earlier time. Some had plank floors,
old display cabinets, and artifacts that could have
been in a museum stacked on shelves along the walls.
I was checking out a place that seemed to be offering
tourists some kind of reenactment of the old days
when a voice from behind startled me.

"So—our paths do come together again."

It took me a couple of seconds to recognize him,
especially since he was not in the same getup. It was
the mountain man from the rendezvous. Only now,
he had on a worn, Western dress shirt tucked into an

equally worn pair of dark brown slacks. His hair was combed back and fastened with a bit of buckskin. His beard seemed neater than I remembered it, too.

"You work here?"

"I own the place."

"I see. So, you make a living giving out-of-towners a taste of that mountain man stuff?" I said.

He shrugged. "Not exactly, but we all have to make a living."

I couldn't resist taking a little jab at him. "Will there be some venison stew on the menu tonight?"

He shook his head. "I savor the special meals when life provides them. Not every night offers such comfort as a good venison stew."

He still sounded the same way he had at the rendezvous. Maybe this was the real him, and not his rendezvous act.

He cocked his head and squinted at me for a minute, then his expression relaxed and he waited. I stood there, wondering what he expected from me. After another bit of time, he smiled and spoke again.

"So, you're on a mission of some sort?" he asked.

I thought about my agreement with Lucinda. "You're pretty good," I said.

"Then tell me. What undertaking keeps you here in our fair town?"

"Murder," I said.

His eyes popped like a pair of flashbulbs.

"Long story," I said. "As you probably know, a young girl was killed just before I rolled into town."

He nodded, continuing to stare at me.

"I was the one who found her body."

"Ah.

"The police thought for a while I might have had something to do with it. I convinced them I didn't, but maybe that's just for the time being."

He grinned. "At the rendezvous you appeared pre-occupied, but relaxed, casual, out for a stroll to enjoy the sights. Now, you have energy, purpose, eagerness. You show impatience to be doing something, ergo you have a mission."

I laughed, "I did agree to do one of the officers a little favor."

"That confirms it, then. You are on a quest."

"A quest?"

He nodded. "To seek justice regarding the young girl's murder, and assure your own state of freedom," he said.

"I guess you could say that. Although, being on a 'quest' sounds too fancy for what I'm doing."

The mountain man grinned, obviously enjoying his little guessing game. He stuck out his hand.

"My name's Rudy," he said.

We shook hands. His grip was firm, confident.

"I should probably just ask you who killed that girl," I said. "You could fill me in with all the answers."

"Hah! I would never take someone's quest away from them. It would be cheating them of their destiny." He grinned at me, and changed the subject. "And what is your usual occupation, when you're not involved solving a murder?"

"I'm a blaster. I blow things up for a living."

He barked a loud and throaty laugh. "A blaster!"

"That's right."

"Then it's little wonder you're eager to be on the hunt, impatient. You're used to things happening all at once. I guess you could say 'happening with a bang'."

He laughed at his play on words, and wiped his mouth with his shirt sleeve. He looked at me, and his face settled into that of a contented Buddha, except for the wrinkles and all that facial hair.

"I'm very patient," he said. "I'm an observer of nature's creatures. Including mankind as one of them."

"And good at it," I said.

Chapter Eleven

I LEFT RUDY and continued my exploration of Williams, more aware of the parked cars I passed by than the windows competing for my attention. Not that I expected to find another body, but some things you just can't help doing. When I reached the diner, a few early birds clustered in booths along the wall. The waitress was the same one as before. The counter was empty. I sat down.

"So, what's it going to be, love," Carrie asked.

I gave her my order for chicken-fried steak and mashed potatoes.

"Go see the canyon yet?" she asked.

"No, I went to something called a 'Rendezvous'."

She stopped writing on her order pad and looked at me. "I didn't take you for the Rendezvous type."

I laughed. "Don't worry, I didn't fill out a membership application. Just thought I'd take in some of the local sights."

"I didn't take you for a typical tourist, either."

I didn't know how to answer that one, or how to save my now-tarnished image.

"Seen Daryl today?" I said.

"No, why?"

"Just curious."

She rolled her eyes and took my order to the kitchen. When she returned with my dinner she said, "You two got a thing going?"

"Yeah, it was love at first sight."

She frowned and leaned against her side of the counter. "I'll say this much, he took to you more than I've seen him accept anybody else around here."

"Maybe it's because I'm not."

"Not what?"

"From around here. I guess he likes motorcycles. A lot of the time, people I run into are taken by that open-road, run-wild-run-free kind of thing. They may never do it themselves, but they think they'd like to, so they take an interest in people who do."

Carrie stepped back from the counter, her eyes focused on whatever lay deep in her own thoughts. She was about the same age as Lucinda. She had a pretty face. I wondered if she had children at home too.

"I guess we all dream about being somewhere else, love," she said.

She left me with that thought, and I cut into my chicken-fried steak. At a thousand calories a bite, it was heavenly.

I ate, then hung around the diner, hoping Daryl might still show up. I had a slice of apple pie, and drank too many refills of coffee. Carrie kept me company when she wasn't busy with other customers. Finally, I decided he wasn't going to come in, and I didn't feel like spending my entire night waiting around to see if he'd prove me wrong.

"I gotta pee," I said. I dug into my hip pocket for my wallet. "Can you ring this up for me?"

When I returned from the men's room, I picked up my change and counted off some ones for a tip.

"I guess Daryl's a no-show tonight," I said.

Carrie shrugged. "Can't let it go, can you sweetie?"

"I guess he got me curious with something he said. So, can I believe him if he says he knows about something?"

She shook her head and sighed. "Oh, Lordy. You would ask that... I have no idea what Daryl knows about anything. Sometimes he rants. Most of the time he just mumbles a lot. I try not to get involved. You should try that too. Make life a lot easier for you, believe me."

"Sounds like the smart thing." I grinned at her. She returned it with the kind of smile my mother used to give me when she knew I had no intention of listening to whatever advice she had offered me.

Daryl was a no-show at the diner again next morning. Carrie shook her head the second I started to ask if she'd seen him. I decided to ask her about Ernesto.

"Not much to tell. I don't really know Ernesto that much. Just the things he's told me about where he's from and about his family. That, and I know what he's like when he's around here. He's a worker," she said. "I don't think he'd murder anyone, if that's what you're thinking. That's for sure."

"What sorts of things has he told you about his family?"

She raised her hand to signal an interruption and went to the cash register to ring a customer out. When she returned, she carried my breakfast. The eggs floated in a puddle of re-fried beans, melted cheese and green chili sauce. Life doesn't get better than that. Especially, served with corn tortillas on the side.

"He sends his family in Mexico money all the time. He once asked me where he could find clothes real cheap. He said he was going to buy a bunch of things to send home, or take them there if he got a chance. That's the sort of person I see him as being."

"He's married?"

She nodded. "Got three kids, too. He works up here to support them and helps out his parents too."

"That's a lot to do on the kind of salary I'd guess he makes here."

"That's why he works at the church. With Daryl. He may have other jobs, too, for all I know." She turned toward the pick-up station to take care of another order.

"So, how can I find this church he works at?"

Chapter Twelve

I PULLED INTO the parking lot of the Holiness Pentecostal Church of the Brethren and veered off to my left, making a tight circle to park near the lot entrance. A grey primer pickup started up with a throaty rumble and idled toward the exit where I had just come in. It stopped when it reached a point between me and the church. The windshield was heavily tinted, but the side windows were both down, so I could easily see inside. The driver seemed to be checking me out, but when I climbed off my bike, he gunned the engine and roared out of the parking lot with a loud chirping of his rear tires, leaving me looking at a leather sack hanging from his trailer hitch like a decorative scrotum with a couple of ball hitches in it. I don't know where he got his decorator sense. I guess he thought it looked macho, like peeling out of the parking lot.

There were a couple other vehicles left in the lot, so I hoped I could find someone around with better manners I might talk to. I headed toward the side entrance of the church, checking the place out as I approached. The building was simple in design, but looked nice. A wall of white stucco rose at the front, topped with three arched openings. The center opening held a cross, and a bell was hung in each side opening. It reminded me of early Spanish missions.

I tried the door, but it turned out to be locked. I knocked, but no one answered. I went to the front entrance, and found that locked as well. A kiosk near the entrance gave the times for Sunday services, the name of the pastor, a biblical reference, and the announcement, "God will be in church Sunday, will you?" I wrote down the pastor's name and went back to the side lot where I had left my bike and fired up the engine. I was reaching for the kickstand when the side door opened and a girl in her teens stepped out. She looked around cautiously before closing the door behind her. I turned off the ignition.

The girl was pretty, youthful, thin and wiry, with brunette hair and light coffee complexion. She clutched whatever she was carrying close against her chest. I guess her intended path led past where I was sitting. I wondered if my being there was making her nervous. She hurried along with her chin tucked down, and I wrestled with whether I should ask her whether anyone else was inside. She was probably about the same age as the girl whose body I found in the car trunk. I decided to let her go about her business without doing anything that might scare her. She kept her eyes on the sidewalk ahead of her as she passed in front of me. I pretended not to be interested in her. When she got a few feet past me, she surprised me by speaking out in a soft, but clear, voice.

"I like your bike," she said.

I turned my head. "Thanks."

She had stopped walking, but hadn't turned all the way around to face me, and she still held tight to the object in her arms.

"You like motorcycles?" I said.

She nodded her head slowly behind a quiet smile.

"I've never had a chance to ride on one—my father would kill me—but, I've always wanted to."

"They can be fun. Is there anybody else around? I was looking for someone named Daryl King. I was told he works here."

Her startled frown was accompanied by a quick shake of her head and a mumbled excuse that she had to go.

I watched her dart off down the sidewalk. I assumed she must know about the murder, and so she might feel leery of strangers. After she disappeared down the street, I knocked on the door of the church again, and got the same results. No one answered. I decided to head back to the campground.

Later, I took out the info for the church that I'd written down and punched in the phone number. A woman's voice answered.

"Hello?"

She sounded old.

"Hello, I'm looking for Pastor Martin. Is he there?"

"Well, yes he is. May I say who's calling?"

I gave the woman my name and listened to her walking down what must have been a hallway, then listened as heavier steps returned. A man's voice came on.

"This is Pastor Martin; how can I help you?"

The voice was deep and rich.

"Hello, Pastor. Sorry to disturb you. My name's Robert Navarro."

I leaned back against the picnic table I was sitting at, as though about to have a nice, intimate conversation. "I was by your church a little while ago, but nobody seemed to be around that I could talk to. I understand Daryl King works there part time."

There was a long pause.

"What did you say your name was?"

I repeated it. I could hear my pulse pounding in the silence that followed.

"I don't recognize your name. Is this church business?"

"Not church business, really. I met Daryl the other day, and was hoping I might connect with him again. Someone told me he has a part time job there. Do you know how I can reach him?"

The line remained silent, except for his breathing. I watched a squirrel work its way down a nearby pine tree, then hop over close to the table.

"Pastor Martin... ?"

"Exactly what did Daryl say to you?"

Chapter Thirteen

IT WAS SUNDAY. The air was warm and dry. I had on my best clean shirt, something that's a luxury on a motorcycle trip. Overhead, the sky was a deep blue dome, making it seem reasonable to assume it might connect with heaven itself, if the stories were true about there being a heaven. I eased into the parking lot of the Holiness Pentecostal Church of the Brethren. When I reached the far side, as far away from the church building as I could get, I shut off the engine. After all, I didn't want my straight pipes making a disturbance. I was still curious to nose around, since Daryl and Ernesto both worked here and I hadn't seen Daryl at the diner.

Pastor Martin hadn't given me any information about Daryl, but I can't say I blamed him for that. I can't say he warmed up to me during the course of our phone conversation either. I kind of hoped he didn't remember who called, now that I had decided to pay the church a visit.

Inside, stained glass windows lined the walls, with sunlight illuminating religious scenes. Double rows of polished wood pews faced the pulpit. It all looked the same as other churches I'd been inside of, except for two ushers, both heavily muscled. One was red headed, and in the shafts of sunlight spilling through the windows, it made his head appear to be glowing. He alternated between putting on his Sunday smile whenever he seated someone, and frowning like a secret service agent as he surveyed the crowd rest of the time.

The other usher maintained a cast iron stare throughout. He looked familiar. His head was shaved, and a tattoo peeked out above the collar of his shirt. He was better dressed than when I last saw him, when he checked me out in the parking lot then took off in a shower of gravel. Showing people to their seats, now? A bouncer? Maybe his job was throwing out anyone who talked during the sermon, or didn't sing loud enough.

I found a pew and sat down on my own, then looked around. A list of hymns was posted on the wall in front. I looked up the first one in a little hymnal I found in a holder fastened to the back of the pew in front of me. Of course, I didn't recognize the hymn, and don't know how to read music for that matter, but I decided I could stick to the words and fake my way along with the melody if anyone sat near me.

I was impressed at the number of young families attending the service. What little experience I could draw on would have led me to expect mostly old people. I've always had the impression most people are too busy to do the church thing every Sunday, unless they've reached that point in their lives when they might want to get things sorted out before it's too late. Not here, though. The congregation was a mixture of everybody.

A boy about six or eight, two rows in front, stared at me with one of those zombie looks that kids seem to enjoy putting on. I winked at him, but left my own expression blank. His younger sister threw me a dimpled smile, as she snuggled next to their mother. The father turned slightly, caught me out of the corner of his eye and frowned, then gave a quick nod, as though he had found himself being unfriendly—not proper Christian behavior for a Sunday. The father wore a light tan suit, and the congregation seemed about equally divided between those with suits and men wearing just slacks and shirts. I was the only one in jeans that I could see.

A door opened at the back of the stage, and a slight-built man I'd put in his early thirties walked to a podium off to the side. Behind him came a group of young women wearing powder blue robes. I recognized one as the girl who liked motorcycles. The rest were in their late teens, with more makeup than I would have expected for members of a church choir, but pretty nevertheless. I could sense a hush coming over the congregation along with the rustle of people changing their positions, picking up and opening hymnals, and ending whatever conversations they had been having.

"Our first hymn for the day is number six-fourteen," the man at the side podium said.

More scurrying, and the sounds of people flipping through pages in search of the right one. The organist sounded a chord, held it for a minute, and then began playing. Everyone joined in with a lot of enthusiasm. I held the hymnal opened in front of me and tried to move my lips along with the music. The people sang with more volume and enthusiasm than I'd expected. When I've been in church, everyone acts like they haven't a clue as to how to sing and feel embarrassed. I could relate to that. But, these people sounded like they were having a good time. Was that to fool the ushers?

When the first verse came to an end, I started to relax, but everyone else kept going until they'd finished all four verses. The man who'd announced the event beamed at the women of the choir as they seated themselves at the side stage. The other guy, the choir director, seemed to be giving him a disapproving look. The ushers had disappeared, so I sat back and tried to relax. We didn't have long to wait. It turned out the first guy, still on-stage also took care of reading scripture, which followed the first hymn.

When he finished the reading, there was another short hush, and then a man I assumed to be Pastor Martin, dressed in a blue suit with a pale yellow shirt and dark necktie, entered from the same side door, and strode to the pulpit in the middle of the stage. He was hefty, easily over two hundred pounds, and all muscle. His hair was thick and wavy, brown, and looked styled rather than cut. Gold rimmed glasses and a heavy gold wristwatch with a gold band completed his outfit. His voice was warm and rich, not at all hesitant or suspicious, as he had sounded over the telephone. His sermon seemed to reflect thoughts that were on his mind, not something he had prepared and memorized beforehand. It focused on the mystery of the loss of loved ones, especially children, and seemed to be an attempt to reassure people that God was still with them.

After services, I waited as the church regulars emptied past the pew in which I sat. Pastor Martin had gone to the entryway. I couldn't see him, but I could hear him talking with people and, I assumed, shaking hands as they filed out.

A couple of other late-leavers stopped at the end of my pew. They came across as eager to recruit me to the fold. The woman clutched the man's left arm, but not in a dependent way, more like steering him. He shook my hand and introduced himself. I'm bad on names, and didn't catch his.

"I'm only visiting," I said. "Just here for a few days."

"You really should join us for coffee and donuts, anyway. We're delighted to have out-of-town guests." They said it almost in unison. He had not yet let go of my hand. He seemed desperate to be friendly. His wife seemed more self-confident. I'd bet she was the kind of woman whose kitchen always smells good and kids are always welcome, while she uses her discussions with them to gather tidbits of gossip about their parents. I guess I'm not the trusting type. We had a lady in our neighborhood like that when I was growing up—in a family of alcoholics. Still, it was tempting to take up their offer, so I said I'd tag along.

"It's in the basement," she said. "We just go around to the back of the building. You just follow us."

On the way out, the couple stayed in line to speak with the pastor. It was clear, I'd have to, too. We edged into the foyer. The organ music stopped. The two ushers/bodyguards stood at either side of the exit keeping an eye on the moving line. Pretty soon, it was my turn.

"Nice sermon, Pastor Martin," I said.

He took my hand firmly, not like a limp fish.

"Good to have you with us this morning."

His voice was warm, his smile broad. His manner somehow gave off a sense of command, although I could read a question in his gaze behind the official smile.

"I don't believe we've had the pleasure of having your company here before," he said.

Might as well get it over with. "My name's Robert Navarro," I said. "We spoke on the phone."

His grip froze.

I pulled my hand loose. "I guess I was hoping I might run into Daryl here. I guess he didn't make it to church this morning."

Pastor Martin's face hardened. His hard-focused stare had the effect of shutting down the friendly buzz that otherwise percolated throughout the entryway. The couple that had invited me to donuts and coffee tucked their heads and scurried through the doorway, suddenly looking eager not to be associated with me.

The pastor finally spoke up.

"Leave Daryl alone."

"What?"

"You heard me. Leave Daryl alone. None of this is your business."

Out of the corner of my eye I could see the bodyguards continue to watch us closely. Pastor Martin turned and walked out the door. I followed along, letting him gain some distance as we passed through the doorway. Without having yet caught any glimpse of Daryl, and with the pastor being so hostile, I was having second thoughts about the donut thing. I had decided to give that idea up when someone coming from behind nearly bumped into me. We both stopped and hurriedly offered apologies for the near collision, then she reached out and grabbed my elbow.

"Come along," she said.

CHAPTER FOURTEEN

THE WOMAN PULLING me by the elbow was in her late forties-early fifties, and wore a light yellow, calf-length dress. She looked like the kind of woman who might serve tea in fine porcelain china.

"I was behind you in the reception line and heard Pastor Martin's comments," she said. "He's not normally so abrupt with people."

"I'm sure," I said.

"No, I really mean that," she said. "Pastor Martin has helped a lot of people, and brought a goodly number of new members into our church, a number of them motorcycle riders like you."

She looked up at me and smiled sweetly.

"What made my case so different?" I said.

"Pastor's been under a lot of stress."

She eased off the pressure on my arm and glanced downward. "Such a terrible tragedy—poor Sherri."

Then she looked up at me again, a look of grandmotherly understanding and compassion on her face. "We've just lost someone to a terrible murder. One of our young parishioners was killed this past week. Such awful business."

She sighed. "I don't know if you could have been aware of that," she said. "It's had a big effect on all of us though, especially Pastor Martin. I hope you'll forgive him for being so rude."

I nodded to let her know I could be forgiving.

"And Ernesto…" She gave a quick shudder. "He's been arrested by the police. Evidently, they think he did it. Ernesto helps Daryl with the grounds, you know. Well, I guess you wouldn't know… But, he works here, although he's not one of our church members."

I looked around at the plantings along the sides of the parking area "Nice flower beds. Daryl the one who takes care of them?"

She smiled. "Oh, Daryl does lots of things. He's a real handyman. If anything needs attention, Daryl's the one to talk with. I don't think Ernesto quite has Daryl's skills yet, but he's learning. Are you a friend of theirs?"

I shook my head. "I've never met Ernesto. Just Daryl. At a diner in town, the other day."

She held her smile, giving me time to finish whatever I wanted to say.

"That was the day after I… the day after that girl's body was found," I said

She nodded soberly. "Absolutely lovely young girl, poor dear. She belonged to our Gospel Youth Group. Her mother, Beth, plays the organ for us. I fill in sometimes, when they need me. Like today. We couldn't expect Beth to feel up to playing just yet. Not after what happened."

I tried to look respectful. Not that I didn't feel for them and their loss. I felt even more sadness for the girl, especially when I was slammed with a flashback to remembering her face in the car trunk. The anger I felt then, surged up again from the pit of my stomach. I tried not to let it show.

Someone else, apparently heading for the donuts, passed us. It was the thin man who read the scripture.

"Hi, Amanda. Coming down for coffee?"

"Be there in a minute, Thomas."

I noticed she frowned a little as she spoke.

"That's Thomas Hansen. He's our deacon."

She smiled in a vacant, but forced, manner, as though gathering her thoughts on the one hand, and working beyond some of them on the other. I got the feeling she and the deacon weren't best of friends. Then she looked back at me as though offering a prompt for me to get on with my story.

"I met Daryl at a diner in town, the day after the murder. I was hoping I could talk with him some more."

"With Daryl?"

"Right."

"You mean about the murder?" she said.

"Well, that was part of our conversation."

"Well, that's strange. I wouldn't think someone... not from our community... would be that interested. I mean... you hear about terrible things happening all the time. All over the place."

"I didn't just hear about it. Actually, I'm the one who found her body."

"Oh, my goodness! I see, then."

She looked genuinely horrified at the mention of my finding Sheri's body.

"And Daryl...?" she said, recovering a little.

"We just got to talking."

She cocked her head to the side and seemed to give my comment some thought.

"You aren't thinking our Daryl is involved in Sheri's murder in some way, are you?" she said.

"No, no. Nothing like that," I said.

"Oh. That's good." she said.

I stuck out my hand. "My name's Robert Navarro. Friends call me Bobby."

She took my hand and gave it a little squeeze rather than a handshake.

"I'm Amanda Trainer."

The deacon had gone ahead inside the room with the donuts. Amanda continued her self-introduction, as the fragrance of coffee and pastries drifted up to greet us.

"Mostly, I look after the vestments," Amanda said.

I had no idea what "vestments" were.

"I only play the organ on occasion."

I smiled. I guess she forgot she had already told me that.

"Daryl can be a little different, sometimes," she said. "But I think he has a good heart. It's interesting that you two hit it off. People sometimes see him as someone they should disregard. I can't say I agree, though. Not at all."

The jumbled voices of the crowd already gathered in the coffee room closed in around us as we entered. Everything was painted in fresh pastels. The light blue walls were decorated with artwork that had to have come from children's classes. Child-sized tables and chairs were scattered around the room in small clusters, now interfering with the efforts of people standing in small knots and attempting to talk over the general noise. A long table covered with a plastic cloth stood against the far wall, and opened boxes of donuts explained the crowd being denser in that section of the room. A coffee urn, paper plates and several stacks of Styrofoam cups sat at one end. Amanda escorted me to the table.

"Is there anything else I can help you with?"

"No. Thanks. You've been great. It was nice meeting you."

Amanda turned her attention to a selection of filled donuts and leaned over them, rubbing her hands together in anticipation. I poured myself some coffee, grabbed a maple glazed donut and looked around at the crowd. The choir members clustered in a corner away from the snacks table. They were all busy chatting with each other, except for the girl I had seen before who liked my bike. She stood next to the others, eating a donut and looking like she was trying to appear a part of the group, but wasn't. I sensed movement at the entryway and turned to see another latecomer had just shown up. It was Daryl.

My first impulse was to squeeze through the crowd and try to get over next to him. Then, I decided to give him a couple of minutes, thinking he would end up at the donuts and coffee if I just let him. I think he would have, too, except he was intercepted by Pastor Martin, who leaned close and said something in his ear. Daryl gave a quick glance in my direction, then nodded toward the pastor and went back outside. I tried to follow, but the kids' tables and chairs and all the people milling about made the going too slow. When I reached the doorway, a now-familiar voice rang out behind me.

"Come back and visit us again sometime, dear. You're always welcome."

I glanced backward and saw Amanda. I waved at her and stepped outside.

"I might just do that," I thought to myself. A really stupid plan of sorts was beginning to take form in the back of my mind from something I had seen in the handout for the service, one that would make it likely we would see each other again.

CHAPTER FIFTEEN

DARYL WAS EATING breakfast when I got to the diner next morning. He sat on the stool at the short end of the counter, looking leaner and more intense than when I saw him throwing knives at the rendezvous. He was making an elaborate ritual of putting jelly on his toast. I sat down one empty stool over.

"How's it going?" I said.

For a moment, he looked as if he was puzzled by who I might be. I thought it was an act. Then his expression cleared, like he wanted me to think he suddenly figured it out.

"Oh, hi. How come you're still here?" he said.

"Police told me I should stick around."

Carrie came by, and I put in an order for eggs and hash browns with sausage and coffee.

"So, you and Ernesto work at the same church?"

A look of suspicion flashed across his face.

"I was there, Sunday. I saw you, but didn't get a chance to catch up and say hi before you took off," I said.

His eyes narrowed. "Yeah, I saw you there, too. How come you showed up at church? Pastor Martin was afraid you might be trying to cause trouble."

"Pastor Martin's the suspicious sort," I said. "Actually, I just thought I'd check it out, and I was kind of hoping I might bump into you again. Our waitress, Carrie, told me you have a part time job there."

His eyebrows bunched into a frown.

"You said you were hoping you'd bump into me again? How come?"

"You got my curiosity up the other day. With that stuff you said."

"What stuff?"

"About the murder."

"Oh."

He frowned and raised his coffee mug. His hand was a little unsteady. He slurped some coffee.

"You said you know Ernesto didn't do it—because you said you know who did."

He set his mug down on the counter, sloshing some of the contents over the side. His jaw muscles twitched as he clamped his lips together.

I thought I'd better back off a little. "So... you and Ernesto pretty good friends?"

He shrugged. "We work together. Used to work together. He's fucked now. Stuck in jail with no money. They probably think he'd take off if they let him have bail anyway."

"Would he?"

He nodded, then shot me a quick, appraising glance.

"Probably," he said. "I wouldn't blame him, either."

Carrie returned with my coffee, and I took a sip. Good and strong, just what I needed.

"I found out the victim, Sheri Norton, was a member of the same church where you two work," I said.

He hesitated. "Lots of people are."

"Right...."

I watched him heave a forkful of scrambled eggs and potatoes into his mouth.

"I don't even know half of them," he said, struggling not to lose any of what he was chewing.

"People there seem to know you."

He shrugged and used his fingertip to catch a bit of food that had escaped.

"The woman who plays the organ said she knows you."

He looked puzzled.

"...Mrs. Trainer?" I said. "Amanda?"

"Oh. Yeah, I see her around all the time. She's okay. Pretty nice, actually."

"That's the impression she gave me," I said.

I let him work on his meal while I started on mine. The eggs were not done as well as I like, but I soaked up the yolks in the potatoes and managed not to spill anything down the front of my own chin, or onto my tee shirt. Not a feat I take for granted, by the way. Daryl relaxed a little. I decided to push again.

"So... you said you knew who killed her. Said it was just like the last time. What did you mean by that?"

He tensed again and swallowed before answering.

"I just meant I know Ernesto didn't do it."

"Oh...?"

He glanced at me out of the corner of his eye. I could tell his mind was working in overdrive.

"I was just saying... you know... some poor bastard no one cares about gets thrown in jail," he said. "And the real murderer goes free. That's happened before. Happens all over the place."

"I hear you."

He took another bite.

"Did you know her? The girl who was killed? Were you friends, or something?" I asked.

The skin on his forehead knotted up again. He gave a quick shake of his head.

"No," he said.

I didn't believe him, at least about not knowing her, but rather than keep pushing, I backed off, taking a moment to look over the breakfast crowd, while processing his denial. The place had filled, and there was a racket of clanging platters, cooks filling orders and people talking over each other. The warm smells of bacon, sausage and pancakes, with a strong accent of artificial maple syrup, hung everywhere. I looked back at Daryl. He was staring at his plate, but I didn't think he was seeing what was on it anymore. He swirled his fork around and occasionally poked at his food with nervous jabs. I wondered what visions were occupying his thoughts.

"Look," I said. "I see that poor girl's face in my mind every time I shut my eyes and try to go to sleep. I never met Ernesto, and I haven't made up my mind if I care what happens to him or not. The cops hauled me in and grilled me before they got to Ernesto and you, and for all I know they might change their minds and come for me again. I'd like to learn whatever I can while I'm still on the outside. Not that it will do any good if they do pay me another visit. But, I'd like to know."

He mulled over my comments while staring hard at the space just above his plate. I gave him a minute, then went at him again.

"So, do you know anything about who did it, or not?"

"Nobody believes anything I say around here anyway. They think I'm nuts. I guess they're right, too. I probably am nuts. And, if I go back and talk to the police, they'll think I did it, and try to work a confession out of me for something I didn't do. I don't want to go through that, man. I can't. I can't do it."

"I'm not the police. Tell me."

His expression turned somber, "I don't know you, either. You might be like all the rest. Besides, I didn't tell you anything before, you just overheard me say something. You don't even know what I meant by it."

I lifted my coffee mug, giving some thought to telling Lucinda I wasn't going to be able to get anything more out of Daryl and calling the whole thing quits. Of course, I knew that wouldn't be easy either. I wasn't kidding Daryl about not being able to get that murdered girl's face out of my mind.

Daryl looked like he was trying to figure out where to go next, too. He twisted around on his stool, then spotted my motorcycle through the window. I remembered him commenting on it before.

"I ride too, you know."

"I didn't know," I said.

I stood to get Carrie's attention so I could pay my bill. Daryl swiveled his seat to face me.

"You leaving?" he asked.

I shrugged my shoulders. He looked suddenly desperate.

"That woman you talked to? Mrs. Trainer? She knows all sorts of things, you know."

I pulled my wallet out and laid some bills on the counter.

"What things?"

"About everything that goes on there."

"And why should I give a shit about what goes on at the church?"

He looked puzzled.

"Because that's where it all happened," he said. "That's where Sheri died."

Chapter Sixteen

AFTER BREAKFAST WITH Daryl, I went back to the campground. I needed to get my head together. Maybe Daryl really did know what happened—maybe not. Maybe he saw it happen, and maybe he was part of it. Maybe too, he was just nuts, like he said himself.

My encounters with Daryl had been interesting, I had to give him that much. Supposedly, Daryl had a problem talking with people. Maybe it was a matter of trusting them. A lot of people have that problem. I wouldn't blame him for not knowing where he stood with me. We had only talked a couple of times. We weren't what I'd call friends. I was just trying to get him to tell me what he knew about the murder. With that in mind, why should he trust me? Of course, the reason I was doing this whole thing, was because he seemed to trust me, at least a little. So far, all I had been doing was hanging out at the diner where he seemed to be a regular, and nosing around the church where he worked. I reminded myself I had stopped off in Williams to visit the Grand Canyon. Maybe I could interest Daryl in taking a ride with me, like out to the Canyon, and we could yak some more. He said he rode, so it seemed worth a try. Too bad I hadn't thought of it at breakfast. Well, next best thing seemed to be to drop by the church again. Maybe I'd catch him at work. Also, I might see Amanda there.

Daryl had suggested I talk more with her, but I had to wonder what she'd tell me. Hadn't she talked with the police?

As before, there were a few vehicles in the parking lot, but I didn't see Daryl or any other motorcycles. I tried knocking on the side door. This time, I heard foot-steps coming toward the entrance. Hopefully Daryl was working inside.

As it turned out, the person who opened the door was the guy who read scripture and sort of got things started for Sunday service. The one Amanda had re-ferred to as the deacon.

"Is there something I can help you with?" he said.

His voice was hesitant, and a little unfriendly. He frowned, like he would like to confront me, but was afraid to let me get too close at the same time. Must be hard, trying to be the pastor's understudy. Martin was a pretty good-sized guy, and hardened. The dea-con was not either. On impulse, I decided against ask-ing for Daryl this time. His name seemed to get people worked up too easily.

"I was wondering if Ms. Trainer might be around," I said.

"What do you want with her?"

"I just wanted to talk with her."

"Well, you won't find her here. She's not in." He took a step back, holding the door ajar, but only bare-ly. I wasn't willing to give up yet.

"Does she usually practice her organ playing on the same day each week?"

After some hesitation, he opened the door a little wider and leaned forward again.

"She doesn't have any regular schedule that I know of. She comes whenever she feels she needs to."

I decided to wait for more information and hope he would cough something up. My tactic worked.

"Amanda's not our regular organist, so she doesn't practice every week. She does have other duties, so I suppose you could say they impose a schedule of sorts."

I had noticed a very slight lisp in his voice, like something that would have been a problem while he was growing up, but barely noticeable now. I raised my eyebrows and waited again.

"She takes care of the vestry materials," he said.

He gave me a know-it-all smile and opened the door wider again, evidently feeling more in control of things as he launched into an explanation of what that meant.

"Vestry materials are the things used to drape the pulpit, serve the sacrament, and things like that. You might say she takes care of the laundry."

He accompanied his explanation with a mixture of a snort and a chuckle. I took that to mean he didn't think her contributions were worth much.

I nodded all the same.

"That means she has to be here some time before Sunday services, and right afterward—to clean up."

"Okay, and sometimes she practices the organ," I said.

"Yes. She does."

I nodded.

He smiled. "When I think about it, she does practice quite often, and, I must say, she's coming along quite nicely."

He looked pleased with his latest comment.

"I take it you're here a lot yourself," I said. "Maybe you could help me with something."

His facial muscles relaxed, as though my interest in him was now perfectly understandable. "If I can," he said.

"You might be able to, you got things rolling the other day... for Sunday services."

He smiled his appreciation for my noticing.

"I'm the deacon. I'm always the one who—get things rolling as you put it."

He gave me a big, self-satisfied smile. I still had no idea what a deacon was, but decided to try giving him more opportunity to impress me.

I stuck out my hand. "My name's Robert Navarro. And, you are?"

"Thomas," he said. "Thomas Hansen."

He shook my hand, without any strength, but not like a dead fish either, just without enthusiasm.

"I was wondering," I said. "Was the girl who died, Sheri Norton... was she in the choir?"

He seemed to weigh his answer carefully, and with a return of suspicion. "Why on earth would you be interested in that?"

"Well, it's kind of a long story," I said. I explained that I had been the one to find her body, and told him I'd been having trouble getting over that experience.

"I just thought it might help if I found out a little more about her, got to know her a little better. What kind of life she'd had, while she was alive to enjoy it. Find out if she had friends, felt like she belonged somewhere. That sort of thing."

A mixture of reactions to all I had just said, played out on his face while he studied mine. After a minute or so, he seemed to reach some kind of position.

"I'm sorry you had to go through that," he said. "I can imagine how difficult it must be for you to get beyond it."

He looked at me with an expression of understanding and sympathy. "All I can say is, she came from a very nice family, was well-loved by everybody, and will be missed as a member of our church. And, yes, she was a member of our choir. She had friends in the choir, and I'm sure she had friends in school."

I looked down at the entryway that still separated us. An ant was trying to get inside. I wondered if it would make it. Probably easier than me.

"The day she was killed... was that a choir practice day?"

He shook his head. "No, we didn't have practice scheduled for then. I remember seeing her, though. Perhaps she was here for something else. Her mother is our regular organist."

I thanked Deacon Thomas for talking with me. "I'm glad she had friends," I said.

I turned and waved over my shoulder as I started toward my bike. After a couple of moments, I heard Deacon Thomas close the door. As I reached my bike, I noticed the bigger of the two bodyguards, the one with the grey pickup who had checked me out the first time I was here, standing at the corner of the church. It seemed likely that he'd been listening in on my conversation with Deacon Thomas. I wondered why he'd be so attentive. Our eyes locked for a minute. When I started my bike up and glanced his way again, he had disappeared somewhere around the back of the church.

CHAPTER SEVENTEEN

I HAD RECONNECTED with Daryl, my prime objective, and I had made a start on learning something about Sheri Norton. I hadn't been able to ask Daryl if he'd like to take a ride, but, with so much accomplished, there was no reason I shouldn't go out to the Canyon myself. It would be a good way to spend the afternoon.

I started the engine, feeling a sudden enthusiasm for taking a break. There didn't seem much else I could do at the moment, and I hadn't been to the South Rim in a long time. I pulled out of the parking lot and turned down the street in a direction I thought would get me to highway sixty-four, leading to the Canyon. Someone else had come out of the parking lot right behind me. In my rearview, I saw it was a pickup, and it looked familiar. I kept checking my rearview as I drove. The pickup stayed pretty much behind me, but didn't get too close. I caught the highway and kicked up speed, leaving the pickup to fade out of view behind me.

It was a pleasant ride, as I had anticipated. The Ponderosa forests around Williams quickly gave way to high desert prairie, dotted with clumps of cedar or juniper. As I drove on, a line of big, puffy clouds stretching west to east hung low on the distant horizon. I wondered if they might be the result of thermal updrafts from the Colorado River. That led me to wondering about the reactions of early visitors to the area when they came upon the Canyon, as well as the reactions of the first of the ancient ones. Did they get tipped off to the possibility of something lying on the horizon by similar lines of clouds? I wondered what they felt when they finally reached the canyon and saw what lay before them.

Of course, there are no such surprises awaiting modern travelers. We take a highway because it promises it will carry us to where we want to go. And, as if that weren't enough, billboard signs along the way make it clear that the Canyon and all the gift shops and tourist traps we could ask for await us just down the highway. Oh well....

Actually, I felt pretty lucky. I had the highway to myself, in spite of the popularity of the Canyon being such a tourist destination. I was in no hurry, and the few cars that did overtake me, were quickly gone and out of my way so I could enjoy the view. After a while, I noticed an image grow from a speck in the rearview, and made it out to be a pickup. It slowed, and stayed well back, only gaining on me again as we approached the village at the rim. Then, it turned off on one of the side roads. I scolded myself for starting to act jumpy. Just because I was sort of playing detective, didn't mean there was a conspiracy of strangers out to get me. I turned my attention to finding a parking area.

The South Rim is a pretty big place, as park facilities go. There are hotels, gas stations, maintenance buildings and so on. I love the view from the overlook there, but at the same time, I wanted to get away from the larger crowds. I found a place I could park and walked the short distance to the viewing area, thinking I would take a quick peek and then drive out to some of the other overlooks.

In spite of the bustle of families, bus tour groups, couples on vacation or honey mooning, or whatever, I couldn't help but drink in the first glimpse of that awesome chasm as though I were the only one viewing it. It's such a breathtaking sight, with all the colors of the desert painting the canyon walls in shades of reds and grays and browns I can't begin to describe adequately. And the thing is, the canyon walls are constantly changing hue as the sun arcs overhead and drops down far away over the desert. Junipers cling to the rim and along the runnels and precipices wherever blown or dropped seeds find a few grains of dust allowing them to take root. Hawks and eagles soar hundreds of feet above the canyon floor, but their altitude still leaves them below eyelevel of someone standing along the rim.

If you are quiet, you might be able to hear the soft moaning of the air currents combing myriad fissures along the canyon walls. Even if you can't hear the winds, you can feel their caress. It lulls you into an inner stillness. After a few moments, chipmunks are likely to come out and try to seduce you into sharing a little something to eat. Blue jays keep more distance, watching and scolding from nearby tree branches, but ever alert for a possible handout. The whole thing is so enormous, and so beautiful, that I always manage to lose myself in the canyon's magic, in spite of the presence of so many others who are present.

I took in a deep breath, filling my lungs with the dry air, perfumed by aromas from the scant vegetation and the canyon walls themselves. The effect was immediate tranquilization. I was calmed, transported to another awareness, like doing meditation. I let my breath out slowly, turned and walked back to where I'd left my bike, unaware now of the others hurrying to catch their first glimpse of the Canyon or to take their next photograph for the folks back home. My intent was to leave them to it, and go to one of the turnouts not far away. As I started up, I noticed the familiar pickup again, as though its driver had been waiting for me. Was I being paranoid?

The first turnout away from the village was not that long a drive, but it had already weeded out most of the tourist crowd, if the number of parked cars and vans n the turnout was any indication. I turned into the parking area and idled toward the far left end, intending to park as far from others as I could. The pickup pulled into the lot behind me. As I approached the end of the lot, the pickup whipped past, nearly clipping me with the rearview mirror on its passenger side.

Reflexively, I tried to veer away from the pickup, but the driver threw it into a tight U-turn and stomped on the gas, spewing a hailstorm of dirt, jagged bits of rock and loose gravel in my direction. I got a blinding, face-full of debris, even though I defensively threw my left arm up to shield my eyes, blinking them shut for an instant.

Fortunately, a part of me was aware that I was also out of maneuvering room. I forced my eyes open, ignoring the flying gravel, and clamped hard on the brake handle. Unfortunately, I was a little off balance, had run out of pavement and felt the tires crunching through the dirt at the parking lot's edge. Next, the unthinkable, and sometimes unavoidable, happened. The bike went down.

I could hear the pickup tires squealing behind me as the driver sped off down the roadway we had just come up. I didn't need to wonder who the driver was. I had been aware of his identity ever since we left the church. It was the bodyguard in the grey pickup with the leather scrotum. I did wonder why he pulled that stunt, though. It was no accident, and was obviously intended as a message of some sort. Go away? Stay away? Or an invitation to look for trouble?

The last thing you want to do, is dump your bike— I mean, the very last thing. It happens sooner or later to anyone, but you never want it to happen to you. At the relatively slow speed I was traveling, it wasn't like I was going to end up with a huge road rash, or turn my bike into a twisted piece of junk. I might well scratch it up, though, or break something. And, even if I hadn't, you never feel okay about dumping your bike, no matter what the cause.

I was mad as hell at the bodyguard for peeling out and spraying gravel all over me too, but when something like that happens, you don't have many options. If you know who did it, you can confront them with it and let them make it right. If they want to. If you think they're interested. I didn't see that option holding any promise.

As another option, you can walk up, next time you see them, and beat the crap out of them—unless they're a member of a gang and you don't care to start a war with the whole gang. In this case, it wasn't a gang I was dealing with, but more than that was hard to say. A preacher? A couple of ushers? It didn't add up.

When the bike went down, I had fallen clear. I scrambled to my feet, still a bit shaken from the spill, and one of my eyes was screaming from bits of dirt and gravel that had gotten underneath my sunglasses. I should have had sense enough to put my goggles back on when I left the village, but since I knew I wasn't going very far, or fast, I thought my sunglasses would be enough. I hadn't counted on all this crap happening. I tried blinking, but that didn't seem to help much. I always carry a canteen when I travel in the desert, so I pulled the water bottle from its canvas holder and poured the semi-warm liquid over my right eye. I blinked again. The water seemed to have helped a little, so I repeated the process, and then wiped the water from my face with a handkerchief.

I looked down at my bike, resting on an angle against the chrome engine guard I had installed as a footrest and in case I ever went down. Good thing I had. At least the engine was protected, even if the engine guard might have been scraped, along with my ego. Next thing would be to get it up as quickly now as I possibly could. I don't know where he came from, but suddenly I noticed a young guy standing just behind me, a little off to the side.

"Hey, can I give you a hand?" he said. "My boss rides a bike, and he'd never forgive me if I didn't help out."

CHAPTER EIGHTEEN

IT WAS WELL into the afternoon the day after my disastrous ride to the Canyon. Lucinda and I were just approaching Grizzly's Café on the main drag. She had turned down my suggestion of having our talk over a beer somewhere else.

"I'd prefer something like coffee, or a glass of iced tea," she said. She made it sound like I should have assumed that in the first place. I thought a cold beer sounded good. Nothing wrong with making a suggestion, I thought. I guess she picked up on my reaction.

"Sometimes a few of the guys get together for a beer and a chance to shoot the shit when a shift is over," she said. "Once in a while I might join them. But, we don't drink on-shift, and my first thought is to always get home in time to give Miguella her supper and spend time with her before she has to go to bed."

I knew I had to appreciate any police rules about drinking on the job, or a single mom's work-and-whatever schedule, so I smiled, said I understood, and held the door opened for her. She led us to a booth inside.

"So, let's have a cup of coffee and you can tell me about what you've been able to learn about Daryl."

She ended with a twitch of a smile at the corners of her mouth. All business. But not quite. Maybe, not quite. Maybe like a trout nibbling at the end of a fishing line, not ready to risk the hook yet, but nevertheless showing some interest in whatever I might have to offer.

I gave her my report on Daryl.

"I tried to get him to open up, but haven't got much out of him yet. He keeps dancing around. I think he's trying to decide if he trusts me anymore than he does everyone else. I tried tracking him down at a church he works. That turned out to be interesting. When I saw him later, he ended up telling me I should go back there and talk to a woman I met who sometimes plays the organ."

"Wait a minute. You went to their church? And started asking people questions about Daryl? What were you thinking?"

I looked at her without answering for a minute, asking myself if I had overstepped my role and just feeling taken aback by her calling me on it if I had.

"It wasn't like that. I learned Daryl had a part time job there. Same with the guy you've got in jail. The victim went to their church, too. I thought it made sense to take a look. It seemed to me, it would give me a chance of running into him again sooner than just hanging out at the diner."

She glared at me, forehead wrinkled like she was trying to decide whether to let loose again.

I was trying to hold my temper, in case she did.

"Whatever," I said. "I don't see how I did anything all that wrong, though. I'm sorry if you think it might get you in some kind of trouble."

She crunched her lips tighter in a look of exasperation. "That's not the point," she said. "I just don't want you to interfere with our investigation, or get carried away. You could end up getting hurt."

I grinned at her. "I don't think Ms. Trainer, the woman I met who plays the organ, is out to get me, but I'll keep an eye on her."

She glared at me, but this time it was with a twinkle in her eyes.

"Seriously though," I said. "I'll try to keep a lid on it. I just thought it would help."

She relaxed and gave me the half-hidden, shy smile that I thought was so cute back in high school. "You still shouldn't have gone there," she said.

I decided I'd better let her in on my introduction to Pastor Martin.

"I also met their pastor," I said. "I guess he shares your view about my showing up on their turf."

I could see her blood pressure heading back toward the boiling point. I didn't let her get far.

"In any case, this woman came up to me, the organist, and sort of apologized for the good pastor's rudeness. She was friendly. We talked a bit. I told her why I was there, and she agreed that Daryl rolls with a few spokes missing. On the other hand, she seemed to think he shouldn't be ignored. Kind of like you, I guess. She doesn't consider him stupid nuts, just a little nuts in other ways. I think she has a soft spot for him."

"So, did you learn anything else from her?"

I shook my head. "Not really, but when I let Daryl know about my meeting her, he told me I should go back and talk with her some more."

She raised her eyebrows. "Why's that?"

"He says she would know about anything that goes on there."

"And...?"

"That was my reaction. But then, he told me that's where Sheri was killed—at the church."

That got her attention.

"He tell you how he knew that?"

"Nope. He went back to being Daryl again. Clammed up and wouldn't say a thing."

She sipped her coffee and looked thoughtful.

"Now, I've got a question for you," I said. "On a slightly different subject. When I saw the murder car parked on the street, I didn't notice any keys in it. I could have missed them, though. Were the keys in the car when it was hauled away?"

She shook her head with a curious, but careful expression.

"Any sign it was hotwired?" I asked.

She shook her head again.

"Well, either somebody had a key, or it had to be hotwired."

"Or Ernesto parked it, pocketed the keys and walked off to work, like we said he must have done. He claimed he thought one of his friends had played a prank on him. You know, new car and all that."

"Yeah, well, that was a bit much for a prank. Steal the car, put a body in the trunk and park it right on the main drag. But, they had to get it running somehow. So, did Ernesto have keys on him when he was picked up?"

She smiled. "He told us he left them in the car."

"Damn," I said.

"So, whoever took it must have taken the keys too. Probably threw them away afterward. But, missing keys still don't let Ernesto off the hook, I guess."

She smiled again. "Afraid not."

The waitress had come up behind and refilled my coffee mug.

Lucinda put her hand on the top of her mug. "Just the check, please," she said.

When the waitress returned, Lucinda picked up the check and wriggled her way out of the booth. "Gotta go," she said. "How about you? What are you up to next, or should I ask?"

"Well, I'm thinking it might be time for me to get religion."

She looked at me with lifted eyebrows.

"They have a Bible study thing," I said. "Might be interesting to join."

Her expression turned thoughtful. "It might be. If that was what you were really doing. And if they let you get away with it," she said.

CHAPTER NINETEEN

I HAVE TO say, I had mixed feelings about going back to the Holiness Pentecostal Church of the Brethren again myself, but I figured I needed to do something. I had managed to make as many enemies there as I had friends. It was clear I wasn't welcome by Pastor Martin and his two goons. On the other hand, Amanda Trainer, the organist, had been friendly, and the deacon had sort of come around. The young choir member who had said she liked my bike, seemed nice. I guessed going back to the church was worth a try.

My plan was to take up the invitation I had seen printed in the little handout they passed around at Sunday service for a Men's Bible Study Group. It had struck me as a good way to gain more access to the church, and maybe more chance to run into Daryl. I thought the idea had the potential to either make things better, or, now that the bodyguard had shown his colors, to make matters worse. I knew from working with demolition, at some point you have to set your charges, lay your fuses, and throw the detonator. It was time for me to do something. Maybe Rudy, the mountain man, was right, I do have an impatient side, and there were things I wanted to find out.

There were more than the usual number of cars in the parking lot when I arrived at the church, and I heard music coming from inside. Choir practice? That could account for the cars. I banged on the side door and waited for someone to answer. It turned out to be Deacon Thomas again. Perfect.

"Can I help you?" He frowned a little. I couldn't tell if it was because he just didn't want anyone banging on the door, or if he was unhappy to see me.

"I hope so," I said with a smile. "I'm not sure who I should be talking to, but you might be just the man."

His frown deepened. "For what?"

"I remember seeing a notice about some kind of Men's Bible Study Group, in the little handout I got last Sunday."

"Yes...?"

"Well, to be honest, I don't have a lot of experience with churches... I was thinking I'd like to get some. I think a little bible study might be just the thing."

He tilted his head and stared at me. "You're saying you're interested in studying the Bible?"

He looked doubtful. I can't say I blamed him. I shrugged. "That's about it," I said.

"Seriously? You want to join our Bible study group?"

"Why not? I've seen a lot of bikers on the road who belong to some kind of Christian thing. They have crosses and things like that on their jackets."

"Our men's group is not a biker club."

"Oh, no, I didn't mean that. I didn't think it was."

He waited.

I looked down at my boots and wondered how far I should go with the shuffle-and-shucks routine.

"Like I said, I don't have a lot of experience with religion. I've never read the Bible. I've been thinking maybe I should learn a little something about it. Talking with you the other day about my problems thinking about the dead girl was kind of helpful. I thought I might try taking another step."

Actually, what I was saying wasn't a complete lie, although I felt a little guilty about playing the sympathy card. I certainly had been having trouble getting Sheri Norton's image off my mind when I had talked with him. And talking with him was helpful in that regard, although for a different reason than I was implying now. That's usually the best way to tell a convincing lie, though. Get as close to the truth as you can, while avoiding it.

To be honest, I had been giving some thought to the big mysteries in life. Wondering what it's all about. Asking why we're even here at all. On the other hand, I can't say I had high hopes I'd find what I was looking for by getting religion either. And, I certainly didn't think Pastor Martin's Holiness Pentecostal Church of the Brethren would help me sort things out, but I didn't intend to go into that with the deacon.

He cocked his head and stared at me, making up his mind.

"Is there someone else I should be talking to?" I said.

He gave me a slow, smile. "Oh, no. You can talk to me. That's perfectly fine. I'm actually the one in charge of the Men's Bible Study group, so you've come to just the right person."

CHAPTER TWENTY

I KNEW I hadn't completely convinced Deacon Thomas of my reason for seeking out the Bible study group, but apparently I had done enough to earn a trial run. Either that, or he figured it might be entertaining to let me flop around in his pond for a while. He told me he was setting up for their meeting, and I could help him.

I followed Deacon Thomas inside and found we were in a broad hallway. To the left were a couple of rooms with closed doors. Another closed room was at the end of the hallway, and to our right was a large room with an open door. Deacon Thomas walked toward the open doorway and entered with a flourish of authority.

The room was empty of any people. Although a mixture of flowery scents floated in the air, suggesting it hadn't been empty long. There were a couple rows of hanging robes along one side and stacks of folding chairs and tables along the wall opposite. A few sweaters and jackets hung on hooks at the end of the wall. I figured the area must be some sort of changing room, obviously used by the choir, which I could hear in the main hall of the church. Busy place tonight.

"We'll need to carry some of these chairs to the vestry office," he said.

I grabbed a chair in each hand. Deacon Thomas took one, looked at me and picked up another, then indicated a doorway at the end of the stacked furniture. He set down one of his chairs, leaned it against the wall and opened the door. I went through ahead of him. I noticed he didn't pick up his second chair as he passed through the doorway.

Deacon Thomas scurried ahead like a mouse on a mighty mission and made a big show of opening the door to the end room and then blocking it open with his body, even though the door didn't appear to be about to swing shut. Once I got inside, I could see it was some sort of office. The entire back wall was lined with bookcases, partially filled with books, but also holding stacks of folders, posters, and other odds and ends. An ancient oak desk presided over the room from its position at the center of the back wall.

Deacon Thomas waved his free arm to indicate the empty area to the front and sides of the desk. "We'll set up here," he said. "Just make an elongated circle. There should be nine of us, including yourself."

I opened the two chairs I had carried in and set them next to each other along what I envisioned one of the longer arcs of the circle should be. He set his chair up in the middle of one of the shorter arcs. I gathered he meant that to be the head of the elongated circle.

"Why don't you start bringing the rest in, and I'll get things ready in here."

"You got it," I said.

I went back to the robing room to get more chairs. On the way back, I nearly bumped into a ladder that had just been set up in the hallway. Daryl stood at the top of the ladder, changing a light bulb. He nearly fell off his perch when he looked down and saw me. I grinned, lifted the chairs I was carrying, as though making a statement that I had a reason for being there, and headed back to the meeting room. It felt like I'd hit the jackpot. It appeared Daryl might be part of the Men's Bible Study group, and likely he'd show up later.

A couple of other people had arrived and were exchanging greetings with Deacon Thomas. I saw them look my way.

"He's going to join us for the evening," I heard Deacon Thomas say, in a quiet voice. "I'll make introductions after everyone else gets here."

I went back for another couple chairs. One of the new arrivals came along. I didn't recognize him, so I stuck my hand out and introduced myself. He seemed to be all smiles and said he was glad I'd be joining them. I grabbed two chairs, and he did the same. I could hear others coming through the outer door as we carried them into the vestry office. When I turned around, I saw the latest arrivals. One was another guy I hadn't seen before. The second was one of the bodyguards. In the lead, was the bastard who had rocked me out at the Canyon and caused me to dump my bike. I let them walk past, and then continued setting up.

The elongated circle of chairs was nearly completed. I started to put one chair at the end opposite where Deacon Thomas had put his. "Pastor Martin sits there," Deacon Thomas said.

I looked at him, confused as to what I was supposed to do in that case. Deacon Thomas smiled.

"He gets the comfy chair," he said. He walked behind the desk, pulled out the wooden office swivel chair bearing a green cushion on the seat and pushed it to where I had tried to set up the folding chair. I put the folding chair on the side, next to it.

When the rest had arrived and taken their seats, Deacon Thomas kept his promise and introduced me to the whole group. Unfortunately, as it turned out, he described me as a biker in search of the Word. The bodyguard who had sprayed me with gravel snorted when Deacon Thomas called me a biker, and said, "Maybe... when he can keep it upright, he might be."

Everyone either turned their heads attentively, or kept them down like they were afraid to get involved. I felt my face flush. After a minute, Deacon Thomas urged everyone to go around the circle and introduce themselves. I learned the bodyguard with the pickup was named Mike, the redheaded one Gary. Actually, when introductions got around to Mike, he didn't say anything, he just grinned. Deacon Thomas did it for him.

"Mike, here, is Pastor Martin's right hand man," Deacon Thomas said. "Along with Gary. Daryl King takes care of anything that needs attention with the building and grounds, and Mike and Gary handle everything else."

Deacon Thomas smiled at me as he finished the introduction, and slipped a quick glance toward the bodyguards, as if checking to make sure his comments had met their satisfaction. The heavyset bodyguard, Mike, threw him a look that said he should shut up. Deacon Thomas shut up.

After that bit, we all waited for Pastor Martin, who arrived a couple of minutes later. A long couple of minutes for me. Also on the down side, Daryl had not joined the group after all, although his ladder had disappeared when I took my last peek down the hall-way.

When he came in, Pastor Martin looked surprised to see me, and not particularly happy about it. Deacon Thomas explained my being there. Pastor Martin took the information in while standing outside the circle of chairs. I could almost hear his mind revving with thoughtful speculation.

Gary sat perched on the edge of his chair, head swiveling between me and Pastor Martin looking for a clue as to what, if anything, he should do. Mike just leaned back against his chair. Finally, Pastor Martin sat down in the swivel chair provided for him and nodded toward Deacon Thomas.

"I've already met our Mr. Navarro," the pastor said. "And, now I'm getting curious to get to know him a little better. So... let's get started, shall we?"

CHAPTER TWENTY-ONE

PASTOR MARTIN'S DECLARATION produced a noisy shuffle and a few attempts at throat-clearing. Those who weren't still keeping their heads down sneaked glances at me, or traded knowing smiles with each other.

Deacon Thomas got up and went to one of the bookshelves against the back wall, and returned with a Bible for me. He had already opened it to some spot I assumed everyone else knew about. As usual, he got the ball rolling. He did it by asking me to tell the group a little about myself.

I started off by saying I was a biker, as Deacon Thomas had pointed out, and was on my way back to upstate New York after visiting a friend of mine out in the Mohave Desert. I didn't know quite how long I expected to be in town, but had been doing a bit of soul-searching, and thought this might be a good opportunity to start getting to know the Bible a little better.

I'd been afraid I might be expected to do a more dramatic introduction of myself. You know, give a little speech about being a sinner, wanting to get saved, or something like that. I'd tried making a few mental notes of things I might say that I wouldn't regret the next morning if that proved to be the case. Most of all, I prayed I wouldn't have to swear to a bunch of holy-this's-or-that's, like I thought some churches made people do. You know, expecting them to confess their new-found salvation, or personal rebirth, or whatever they think got into them.

One of the men in the group asked me if there was anything in particular behind my soul-searching. As I opened my mouth to try responding, the door opened with a faint sound of hinges scraping against each other and in walked Daryl. He mouthed an apology for his interruption and took the remaining seat, taking care not to make any more noise moving the metal folding chair than he could avoid. Deacon Thomas looked at him with disapproving patience written all over his face. Once Daryl had sat down and started fumbling through his Bible, Deacon Thomas spoke up again.

"I'm sure Mr. Navarro's needs are clear to our Lord," Deacon Thomas said. "And, we don't need to insist he share them with us at this point in time. And, I'm just as sure those needs will be met in the Lord's heavenly intervention—whatever that proves to be."

He threw a final disapproving look at Daryl, glanced toward the preacher with a businesslike smile as if to say, "There, that's taken care of," and then turned back toward me.

"Our rules are pretty simple," Deacon Thomas said. "We're here to make a serious effort to bring the teachings of Jesus into our daily lives. We all read a portion of the Bible at home, then discuss it here. In addition, whoever has a problem they're dealing with, or just anything special they want to share, they do so, and the rest of us discuss how it's handled in the Bible.

"So, Robert—can we call you Robert? —we like to be on a first-name basis here. Although I marked the Bible I gave you with the page everyone is prepared to discuss, you won't be expected to take part fully, just yet. We'll let you get comfortable first."

I thanked him for his consideration. I did have one other thing I wanted to say, so I raised my hand like we were trained to do back in school. Of course, back in school I often ignored that rule. This time, I compromised. I raised my hand a little but spoke up without waiting for his permission.

"I'd be just as happy, though Deacon Thomas, if everyone called me Bobby," I said. "Robert sounds like my old man talking, and the 'Mr.' stuff only happens when I'm in some kind of trouble."

The group laughed a bit at that, and seemed to relax a little. Even Deacon Thomas. He smiled and nodded as if to say I had passed his little admissions test—at least for the time being.

"So," Deacon Thomas said. "Does anyone have something they'd like the Lord's help with?"

After a brief pause, Roger, the guy who had helped me carry in the chairs, cleared his throat and spoke.

"My wife Katie is coming up with more than her share of headaches again."

That brought a round of laughter.

"We all have needs," one of the men to my right said.

Gary, one of the bodyguards, chimed in. "I don't even have a wife," he said. "You're lucky."

More laughter, followed by a rapid-fire bunch of suggestions for scripture Roger should read, or read to his wife, such as "Wives, submit to your husbands as to the Lord" and "The husband should give to the wife her conjugal rights, and likewise the wife to her husband." Another one was, "Do not deprive one another, except perhaps by agreement for a limited time." I didn't know if it was real scripture, or just sounded like it, but it seemed to make the point that both Roger and his wife had obligations, and maybe Roger wasn't getting his met.

The rest of the meeting kind of went along the same way, lighthearted much of the time, more serious at other times. It made me think of a bunch of good old boys passing the jug and sitting around a bonfire, enjoying the company, having fun in the moment. There was some competition over the Bible reference stuff. It seemed like someone would gain points for every verse they could cite or quote. Pastor Martin was clearly the leader, and others competed to line up as close to him as they could. Except for Daryl. I couldn't tell if he was behind the others in his memorization, or uncomfortable being a part of it at all. In any event, his only contribution was to nod once in a while at what others said. Mike was another one who did not chime in. I guessed he simply didn't feel any need to.

When it was over, Gary and Roger stayed on to help me and Deacon Thomas clean up, along with Daryl who grabbed a push broom right away. Pastor Martin hung on as well, I guessed to close up shop. I started folding chairs and helped carry them back to the robing room.

Evidently, Gary had decided I was okay. He seemed to believe me to be a genuine new recruit, similar to himself, a biker with a newfound quest. He told me a number of bikers had become interested in the church in the past.

"In fact," he said. "Mike, Pastor Martin and I all rode together back when."

I looked at him, surprised. He smiled as though he had expected me to have that reaction. He explained that none of them had ridden in years, and admitted that he sometimes missed it.

"Some of that life was real good," he said. "But I wasn't. I was real bad. Then I found Jesus, and life is a whole lot better than I ever thought it would be. You stick with the program—the Lord's program for you—and you'll be glad you did."

We chatted on for a while, while we folded chairs and took them into the robing room to stack them against the wall.

"I don't think I've hit it off all that well with Pastor Martin," I said. "For that matter, I be real honest, I had a few misgivings about the way you and Mike came off looking like a couple of bodyguards the first time I came here."

He laughed and shook his head at my description of the two of them.

"We're all a pretty tight little bunch, here," he said. "I sure wouldn't call us bodyguards, but Pastor Martin likes to run a tight ship. That way, nobody comes in here and takes over for their own purpose. Everybody gets what the Lord intends for him, and it all stays good. Once you're accepted, everyone has your back for life."

"Good to know," I said.

"I mean it. We look out for you. Do anything it takes. And don't think we don't have some handy connections." He said it with a self-satisfied grin.

"Is Mike one of them?" I asked.

Gary smiled, but didn't say anything.

A small folding table had stood between the circle of chairs and the side wall near the preacher's desk. Pastor Martin asked us to take it into the robing room while we were getting the rest put away. I grabbed one end and Gary took the other. When we flipped it up to lay against the stack of tables in the robing room, Gary noticed something caught on the underside.

"Whoa, what's this?"

I peeked around my end of the table to see what he was talking about. Pastor Martin looked our way too. I held my end still, bracing the half-overturned table with my leg, while Gary leaned over and eased the object out from where it had been caught between one of the legs and the hinge mechanism for folding them. He lifted the object free, just as Deacon Thomas rushed over to claim it.

"Hey, take it easy, Deacon," Gary said. "You'll break it."

Deacon Thomas started to slip whatever it was into his pocket.

Pastor Martin came over and threw his hand out, palm up. "Let's see that," he said. His voice was filled with authority, and he sounded angry.

Deacon Thomas hesitated, then let the object tumble into the pastor's open hand. It turned out to be a thin, gold chain with a tiny cross on it. "I wasn't going to..."

Pastor Martin glared at him, closed his hand on the necklace and slipped it into his own shirt pocket, "Thank you boys. I'll make sure this gets back to its rightful owner."

Gary and I finished stacking the table against the others.

"What did you make of that?" I said.

"What?"

"That thing about the necklace."

Gary shrugged, looking self-conscious. "Oh, nothing really. Sometimes Deacon Thomas tries too hard. Pastor will take care of it. He can make an announcement in church, or something."

"Right...."

Gary let me know we were finished with our part of the cleanup. As we stepped out into the hallway, Deacon Thomas called out to me. "So, are we going to be seeing you next week?"

I couldn't tell if it was a challenge or an invitation. I pointed toward him with my finger extended like the barrel of a pistol. "I'll be here," I said.

"Don't forget your homework," he said with a laugh. "There'll be a test."

I walked outside, hoping to catch sight of Daryl. I still wanted to suggest a ride together, but I guess he'd slipped out while we were stacking the chairs. He was nowhere in sight in the parking lot. But, when I looked across the lot where I'd left my bike, I saw someone else, the young girl from the choir, standing next to my bike.

Chapter Twenty-two

SHE HAD HER dark hair tied in a ponytail, wore a knit top, jeans and sneakers. In her hands, she clutched a worn-looking manila folder, fat with papers of some sort, close against her chest. Her face looked tired, a little sorrowful.

"I thought this was your motorcycle." she said as I approached.

I smiled at her.

"It's really beautiful." Her eyes caressed the bike with appreciation.

"Thank you," I said.

"Are you really from New York?"

I nodded.

"Wow. That's a long way."

"I guess it is," I said.

"Did you ride all the way?"

I told her I had.

She stepped back, giving me room to climb on. "I'd give anything if I could do what you're doing."

I threw my leg over and settled into the saddle.

"But, like I told you," she said. "My father would kill me if he caught me on a Harley."

"Just a Harley? Or, any motorcycle?"

"Any bike. Harleys mostly, though. His younger brother died in an accident."

"Sorry to hear that."

She smiled and stuck out her hand. "I'm Teresa. Teresa Gonzales."

I shook her hand.

"My name's Bobby Navarro."

Her hand was warm and soft to the touch.

"Aren't you part of the choir?" I asked.

She said she was, and explained that they just had their weekly practice. I told her I was there to check out the men's Bible study group. She wrinkled her nose and gave a quick shake of her head, which I assumed was a negative reaction to what I had just told her.

"You disapprove?" I said.

"Oh, it's not that. It's just...."

The sound of laughter erupted from the other side of the parking lot, near the rear of the church. I looked that way, and saw Mike leaning against a car, talking with Deacon Thomas and the choir director, Ben.

"I'd better leave," Teresa said. She hurried offs without another word.

After a moment, I hit the starter switch and felt the bike come to life beneath me. I raised the kickstand and released the clutch, easing the bike out of the parking lot and into the night that had quietly swallowed Teresa Gonzales.

CHAPTER TWENTY-THREE

I HAD CALLED Lucinda and arranged to give her an update, even though I didn't think I had made much progress. On the good side, she didn't seem discouraged. Maybe it was just me.

"Well, I joined the Bible study group."

"You what?"

"Joined the Bible study group at their church. Like I mentioned. I thought it would give me a chance to nose around and see more of what goes on."

She took in a deep lungful of air, and shook her head.

"Actually, it was an interesting evening," I said.

She threw me a quizzical look, without saying anything.

"When I was there Sunday, I noticed these two guys who looked like they might be Pastor Martin's goon squad. Turned out they're part of the study group, too. I got to talk a little with one of them, name's Gary. He's a real Born-Again. Used to be a biker and a baddass. Found Jesus, and says he's happy as a clam. He wouldn't admit to being Pastor Martin's muscle, exactly, but he painted a picture of a tight organization with Pastor Martin at the head. Everyone does whatever he wants them to, I guess. Gary let me know I could get to be a part of things, if I fit in and didn't cause problems."

"Is Daryl a part of this Bible study group?" she said.

"Yeah, sort of. Looks like he does odd jobs, so he's around there a lot. He was changing a light bulb when the meeting was getting organized. He came in later, but didn't really seem to get involved. Kept to himself, and looked awkward most of the time. I didn't get any chance to talk with him, though. He took off right after the meeting. I wanted to suggest we take a ride together—he's got bike, too."

"Good idea, anything else?"

"Not really," I said.

Then I thought about Teresa.

"I'd just like to hurry up and find out if Daryl knows anything."

"You sound disappointed," Lucinda said.

"Maybe impatient would be a better word."

"Well, hey, you've made a start. Don't forget, you're not flying solo. This isn't even your investigation. It's not even your town. You were supposed to be taking a vacation."

"It's a murder that never should have happened. I just don't want another one... especially if I could have done anything to prevent it."

"And more people should feel the way you do. But these things sometimes take time, and we can't always get everyone we go after. Sometimes, we can't get anyone. That's why you're helping us. We're getting a second look at Daryl King, thanks to what you're doing."

I couldn't help but feel a little better, hearing her encouragement.

"I'm getting a better sense of Pastor Martin and his bunch," I said. "I guess I shouldn't complain. I'd like to find out more how Daryl fits in with all them. I assume they accept him well enough. Some must like him. Maybe if I could learn more about his background I could understand him better and figure out how to talk with him better myself."

You might try talking with his half-brother, Ben."

"Ben?"

"Ben Edwards. He's the church choirmaster. You've no doubt seen him. Maybe he's part of the Bible study group. He owns a used car dealership in town. It would be easy enough to find him."

So, Ben Edwards, choir director, was Daryl's half-brother, and owned Ben's Autos. I thought the name had sounded familiar when introductions were made at the Bible study meeting. A simple enough name for a business, friendly... easy to remember. It was also the name I had seen on the back of the car holding Sheri Norton's body.

CHAPTER TWENTY-FOUR

SOMETIMES YOU CAN tell a lot about a town by its automobile dealerships. The cars on the lot Daryl's
brother owned appeared clean, in nice shape, and
priced between five and ten thousand dollars. Not big
time, but don't kid yourself, you can make a good living off of used cars in that price range. I paused near
a Ford Ranger.

"Thinking about a pickup to haul your motorcycle?
Or are you looking to trade your bike in on a truck?"

I turned around to see Ben standing behind me.

He stepped forward and extended his hand.

We shook.

"I'm Ben Edwards," he said. "Didn't we meet last
night?"

"We did," I said. "At the Bible study meeting."

"Yes. Good to see you again," he said, still grinning
his best five-thousand-dollar-deal smile. It was almost as though he wasn't convinced he'd recognized
me yet.

"That was interesting—the Bible study meeting." I
said. "I've never been to anything like that before."

Ben's smile changed from the used car dealer to
something else, but I couldn't say what.

"I'm sure it will grow on you," he said. "It's a great
bunch of guys, and learning what the Bible can do for
you is a joy that never stops giving."

"Good to hear," I said.

He stood, waiting for me to get around to business.

"You know, I just learned you and Daryl King are brothers," I said.

Ben's expression changed to a look that said he'd had discussions about his half-brother before, and dreaded the thought of having another one. A nervous twitch played at the corner of his mouth, and his eyes darted back and forth, as though checking to make sure no other customers might overhear us.

"We both have the same father. He's dead, though. Died some time ago."

I nodded, while Ben continued to look uneasy, and appeared to be awaiting some explanation for this turn of the conversation.

"I met Daryl the day after I came into town." I said. "At a diner down on the main drag. It was the day after that girl was killed."

He tensed, noticeably.

"We were talking over breakfast, and of course, everyone was discussing the murder. I was interested because the police had already questioned me the night it happened. Also, I was interested because I was the one who found her body in the back of the car belonging to Daryl's friend, Ernesto."

"Oh, I see."

Ben held his hand up for me to stop talking, and jerked his head toward the pickup we were standing next to. He grabbed my upper arm and steered me around to the passenger side, holding the door open for me to get in. I did. He walked around and climbed in behind the steering wheel.

"Maybe you should tell me whatever you two talked about," he said.

"Well, Daryl seems convinced Ernesto didn't do it," I said. "He said he knew who actually killed the girl. Later, he changed his story to claim he just believed Ernesto wasn't the one who did it. I'm trying to figure out which version to go with."

"Go with...?"

"I can't get that girl's face out of my mind. If he does know what happened, I'd like him to tell me."

"So you can do what?"

"I don't know. So I can put it to rest, I guess. The police thought for a while I did it. Then they let me go, told me to stick around, and the next thing I knew they had arrested Ernesto. But, when I met your half-brother, he seemed convinced Ernesto couldn't have done it. So, for all I know, the police will be getting back to me again. If Daryl knows something, it may be important."

Ben took a deep breath and leaned back against the seat. "You have to understand some things about Daryl..."

His eyes bored into mine as though he intended to implant, rather than tell me, whatever it was he was about to say. "My half-brother's always been a little... let's just say, you shouldn't believe everything he tells you."

Ben's face regained some of the salesperson's confidence he'd displayed earlier.

"Why is that?" I asked.

He smiled, and bumped me lightly on the arm with his fist. "He doesn't mean to tell people lies. Not usually, anyway. It's just that... Daryl has difficulty keeping what's real apart from what he wants to believe.... or wants others to believe. Sometimes, he does things to make himself feel important."

After a minute, he said, "Since you've started coming to our study group, trying to get yourself right with the Lord, I feel obligated to give you a heads-up, let you know you can't always rely on what Daryl says to you. That's why I'm telling you this."

"I appreciate that."

A late model pickup with a couple of good old boys rolled into the lot. They got out and started down the row of vehicles.

"I need to let these people know I'll be here for any questions they might have," Ben said.

I nodded.

After a couple of minutes, Ben came back to where he'd left me sitting inside the pickup. He climbed into the driver seat, and turned to face me. "Sure you wouldn't like to take this for a spin? I can promise you, you'll love it."

I smiled and shook my head, then waited for us to get back to our discussion, uncomfortable though it had been for both of us.

Like a lot of people when they feel uncomfortable, Ben needed to fill the silence. So, he talked. About Daryl. About growing up together. While he unloaded, his gaze stayed fixed in the distance, his voice low and thoughtful, like he was sorting through memories, with nothing of the salesperson's cheery banter.

"Daryl's mother used to work for Dad. There was always something about her that seemed to irritate Mom. I was aware of that. Of course, I never understood what it was. Well, not at the time."

He threw me a quick glance. "Dad worked a lot at night. That's the nature of the business. You know?"

I nodded without saying anything. He turned his head back toward the windshield.

"But I don't think Mom liked it that the two of them spent so much time together."

He glanced at me again, his expression a tentative peek to see if I was going to demand more specific information or let the story go the way he wanted to tell it.

I gave him have a slack rein and said nothing.

"After Daryl's mother died, Dad insisted on bringing him to live with us. Mom wasn't happy with that idea at all. I remember they had a lot of fights. Then, one night, Mom came out of the kitchen, where they'd been carrying on with their latest argument. She was crying, but there was just no more fight left in her. You could see it in her face. We took Daryl in, and after that, things were never the same."

He took a deep breath and let it out in a slow release of both air and tension.

"Later, Dad told me Daryl was my half-brother. I didn't really understand what that meant, except I was supposed to... accept Daryl as part of our family. I was supposed to... like him. Worse, I was supposed to take care of him."

Ben balled his right hand into a fist and banged it softly against the dashboard.

"I knew he was just a little kid. Someone else's little kid, as far as I was concerned. The part about Dad being Daryl's father just seemed confusing. I mean, I knew how babies get made, but I just couldn't accept Dad and her doing that. We weren't brothers in my mind, not like I thought brothers were supposed to be. I looked out for him at school, and around the neighborhood, because Dad said I had to. But, I couldn't make myself like him."

"Can hardly blame you for feeling some resentment," I said.

He smiled a little.

"Imagine how my mother felt. She was stuck with raising him. Not only that, but Dad insisted they adopt him, too. It nearly killed her. In a way, it did. Something inside her died after that night they had that argument in the kitchen. And, everything she was before Dad's... affair... wasn't the same after he brought Daryl home."

Ben let his gaze drift over the car lot again, but I could tell he wasn't looking to see whether any other customers needed his attention this time. I think, what he was seeing had more to do with those scenes from a long time ago. After a minute, he took another deep breath and refocused on our conversation.

"I suppose it wasn't any easier on Daryl. I mean, he had to move into someone else's home. My home. With me and my mother. And neither one of us liking the idea of him being there."

"How did your mother handle all that?"

"I guess she did what she had to do. She never said anything in front of me against him. She never talked about his mother and Dad, or whatever."

He paused, and looked off to the side again. "I know it was hard for her, though. She tried to do right by us both, but Daryl always said I was her favorite, and I'm sure I was. After all, I was her real son, her only real child."

He shrugged and paused for a moment. "Daryl was pretty unhappy back then. I think that's why he did such mean things. You know, to get back at us and the rest of the world. Maybe even just to get a little attention."

"What kind of things?"

Ben gave an expansive wave of his hand. "Oh, the kind of things kids sometimes get
into."

I asked him for some examples. He shared a few with me. One was pulling a girl's underpants down. Another claimed he killed a couple of rats one Halloween and hung their bodies on the fence surrounding the school. As Ben's stories wound down, his voice got smaller and he seemed to shrink into himself. After a while, he stopped talking. We both sat there for several minutes. Ben was the one to finally break our quiet.

"I think the only thing Mom had left was church," he said. "Maybe that's why I first joined Pastor Martin's Holiness Pentecostal Church of the Brethren."

He glanced into the distance, as though taking a final look back, then turned to the present. "I'm sorry, but I really should get back to work," he said.

"I appreciate your talking with me," I said.

CHAPTER TWENTY-FIVE

AFTER TALKING WITH Ben, I picked up a six pack of Tecate at a convenience store and threaded my way across town to the campground. Enough for one day. I needed to process some of the stuff I'd heard from Ben. Some of the stories about Daryl were giving me reason for a timeout, and a need to do some thinking.

The day was hot and, for this part of the country, a bit humid. Clouds were building in the north, and the sky seemed heavier, not as blue and fathomless as usual. I hadn't bothered to get a weather report, unless I'm traveling a serious distance, I seldom do in the West. No need. It's almost always warm, clear, maybe with some clouds in the afternoon. Another beautiful day. I'd swear the forecasts were exaggerations written by tourist agencies, if they weren't true so much of the time.

I had half-hoped Jeanine and Ann would be there when I got to the campsite. I felt I could use their company, and maybe some of their brain power. Unfortunately, their rental car was gone, and so were they. I popped the tab on a can and drained most of it in the first two swallows. I felt hungry, so I set the can on the picnic table and scooted over to the camp store, sure they would have something tempting to snack on. Russ was behind the counter. I had the strangest feeling he knew I had an open beer waiting for me that I hadn't bought from him.

"What can we help you with, buddy?" Russ said.

"Just looking for something to snack on."

He waved his arm to take in most of the room. "We have plenty of that. Just look around and find whatever tickles your fancy."

"I'll do that."

"We also have beer in the cooler," he said.

Aha! He did know. I thanked him and walked down the aisle toward some brightly colored boxes on a top shelf. One of them was a box of cheddar biscuits. I grabbed it and headed for the counter. I fished my wallet from my back pocket and dug out a five, holding up the box of cheddar biscuits so he could see what I needed to pay for. Russ took the money without comment.

I was working on my second Tecate when Jeanine and Anne showed up. They climbed out of their rental car, full of smiles and cheerfulness.

"Hi, Bobby. How are you this afternoon?" Jeanine said.

"I'm good. How about you?

I offered them a beer. Anne turned the offer down, but Jeanine accepted with a big show of gratitude. She took a healthy pull on the can and set it on the picnic table.

"You seem preoccupied. Have you been busy helping your friend with the investigation?" she asked.

"Well, I don't know how much help I'm providing, but I guess I've been busy."

"Then, you should feel good." She flashed me a cheery smile, and, at that point, I felt like I must have had a good day, if she thought so. It certainly seemed good at the moment.

On impulse, I asked her if they had plans for dinner somewhere, or if they were eating at the campsite.

"Oh, we have some food we bought, and we are going to cook it here. Maybe we can make a fire, like you had last night."

I told her I was about to get more firewood from the camp store and would be happy to get some for them too.

"Oh, great. I will go with you," Jeanine said.

"You sure? Those bundles of wood can get heavy."

She laughed. "We girls from Norway are very strong. I'll show you how easily I can carry wood." She made a muscle with her arm to show me how strong she was.

I laughed, already looking forward to the evening. "Let's go, then."

On impulse, I glanced above the tree tops as we walked to the store. The clouds I had seen earlier had not made it this far yet, but the sky overhead had grown denser. We paid for a couple bundles of wood and went to the storage shed to pick them up.

After we carried our armloads of wood to the campsite, I offered Anne a beer again. This time she accepted. We all traded small talk, and Jeanine asked if I'd like to join them with whatever I had for a dinner together. Of course, I said yes. We shared our ideas for dinner and I went back to the camp store to buy some canned chili beans to add to the things they had already purchased in town. I picked up an onion as well. Fortunately, I had a couple of jalapeno peppers in my pack; the camp store didn't have any. I took my stuff and headed toward the counter to pay.

As he took my money, Russ seemed eager say something. In a hushed voice, with a quick look around to double check that no one was there to overhear, he asked me if I had everything I needed. I wondered what the hell was going on, shrugged and said I guessed so. He pulled a condom package out of his shirt pocket and held it up for me to see.

"I can sell you a couple of rain jackets for your buddy, if you don't have any. Got to be prepared, you know."

Just what I needed, a horny camp host who wanted to get some vicarious kicks on Route 66 through me. I wouldn't dream of buying a condom off him, if I'd had that in mind. I laid the beans and onion on the counter and said that would take care of everything I needed. Fortunately, another camper came in and kept Russ from going on about the sexual opportunities he wanted to make sure I didn't miss out on. Back at the campsite I didn't give the girls the part about my encounter with Russ.

I'm not particularly fussy about rustic camping. I can cook squatting on the side of a road and eat standing up, if I have to. On the other hand, a few amenities can be pretty nice, sometimes. A friend of mine once gave me a small, vinyl table cloth, about big enough to cover a card table, and told me I was worth some of the comforts and good things in life. I smiled to myself as I pulled the tablecloth from my pack, spread it across the end of the table, and dumped out the supplies I had picked up from the camp store. Actually, given the food spills and bird stains you often see on picnic tables, a tablecloth can be a pretty good idea.

Jeanine and Anne were busy starting the fire. Once it was cheerfully blazing away, I dribbled a little olive oil in a pot, diced a couple of the jalapenos I had, along with the onion, and threw them in the pot. When they were tender, I added the two cans of chili from the store and set the pot on a grate over the fire.

Jeanine and Anne had bought hotdogs and buns. On top of that, they had a bottle of red wine. What could be better?

While we watched the fire burn down to a bed of hot coals, I passed around the remaining Tecates.

It always gets cooler as the sun goes down at this altitude, but the breeze had picked up, and carried a chill that signaled a change in weather. Anne ducked inside their tent and came out wearing a polar fleece jacket and asking if we thought the fire was ready for cooking. Happily, it was.

After our meal, Jeanine and Anne insisted on taking care of dishes while I was put in charge of stoking up our fire again. By then, it was cold enough I had put on a long sleeved shirt and my leather vest as well. Both Anne and Jeanine had added jackets. I wondered how long our campfire conversation would last before the weather sent us inside our respective tents.

Sounds from most of the trailer sites suggested kids had quieted down, or possibly gone to bed, already. Occasional noises from pots and pans clanking together as dishes were taken care of, or a flare-up of laughter over conversations too far away to follow, was a familiar and welcome part of the scene. The orange glow of distant campfires told me adults were still up and enjoying the same idea we had, taking advantage of the campfire while the opportunity remained.

"So Bobby, tell us what you have done in your investigation. I think it's exciting." Jeanine said.

As if adding a sinister punctuation to Anne's question, a heavy gust of wind blew through camp, carrying with a spatter of rain drops. I looked up at the sky. Usually, when it first gets dark in the forest, the sky stays lighter for a while. Tonight the sky was inky black. I studied dark shapes of rainclouds scudding overhead, low and ominous. It didn't look good.

"I don't know about my investigation being exciting," I said "It's come with a fair amount of frustration and confusion, though."

"Confusion?" Anne asked.

I had to laugh at myself. "Yeah, I guess mostly confusion about what I should be doing."

Jeanine's forehead wrinkled. "So, tell us what you have been doing."

"Well, I guess the craziest thing I've done is to join a Bible study group."

They both looked shocked at my comment, and not sure whether to believe I was being serious.

"The girl who was murdered was a member of the church where they have the Bible study thing. The guy they arrested worked at the church, and so does Daryl, the fellow who seemed to know something about what happened. He was the reason I've been helping Lucinda, my friend on the police force. I figured joining the Bible study group might be a way to learn more about what all goes on there, and what kind of people the murdered girls were running into."

"But to join such a group... that seems very...." Anne said. She wasn't able to finish her statement, but the laugh that escaped her made her thoughts clear enough.

"Anne, you shouldn't laugh at Bobby. What he is doing is very courageous," Jeanine
said.

"I know," Anne said. "And I was going to say so, but the idea of a Bible study group possibly being dangerous struck me as being very funny."

We all had to laugh at that one.

"Perhaps they are going to baptize you soon," Jeanine said with a flirtatious grin. "Are there any rivers nearby?"

"Whoa, that's not happening," I said. "I think I used up all my courageousness just joining the study group."

"But if it does happen.... I want to be there when they do it. Don't you have to wear a thin white gown? That would be like watching a wet T-shirt contest for men, wouldn't it, Anne?"

"Forget it, you two. Like I said, it's not happening." I'm sure my face was beet red, but mercifully they didn't keep it up long.

"But, do you really think someone in this group is the murderer?" Anne said.

I shrugged. "That's hard to say."

"I think you must be very careful," Jeanine said. "I don't think you should trust the people you meet at that place."

CHAPTER TWENTY-SIX

A HUGE EXPLOSION of thunder put a quick end to our conversation and sent Anne and Jeanine running to their tent. I threw some water on the fire, even though I was sure the thunder would be followed by enough rain to do away with any threat of the fire getting out of control. Better to be safe than sorry. Another thunder clap and sudden rush of wind told me I'd better get into my own tent. With a quick glance at my bike, I folded myself into the vestibule opening of my tent just as the rain started getting heavy.

The main problem sleeping in tents in campgrounds is, the sites available are usually worn down to giant saucers and you can't pitch your tent on a gentle slope. That means you can end up getting flooded out pretty easily. I have a heavy duty, plastic ground cloth I use with my tent, and I'd set up on the best area I could find. I also raked pine needles together to provide some cushioning and a little extra insulation from ground water if the slope wasn't enough. To increase the odds I'd be all right in a downpour, I scraped a little trench around the perimeter of my tent, right under the rainfly. You're probably not supposed to do that sort of thing in a campground, but I'm pretty good about restoring the site to original condition when I leave, so I gave myself permission. With the rain now coming down in a torrent, I was glad I had.

People expect the desert to be dry. Most of the time, it is. When it isn't, things can get pretty dramatic. I've seen torrential rainfall in a dessert pueblo send a river of muddy water a foot deep down the main street of town. I've even seen that happen in a city of eighty-thousand with pretty good drainage systems. If the ground can't absorb the water fast enough, it has to go somewhere. Even in the high county, like here, a sudden downpour can become a problem, especially in a tent.

The rain and thunder continued for a while, making it clear that the path of the storm plowed right over our campground. I wasn't ready to sleep yet, so I lay there, thinking about my "quest", as Rudy, the mountain man, had put it, and the people I had run into since my arrival. Daryl was something of a mystery. I didn't know what I thought about him yet. Reconnecting with Lucinda had been great, even though the original circumstances were terrible. Jeanine and Ann were fun, especially Jeanine. I felt good whenever I was around her. I guess it was because she seemed able to care about others, but still keep her own thoughts intact. I felt I could trust her.

The storm continued to rage. After a while, I stuck my head out for a minute to watch the show. Lightning flashes ripped the darkness. The line of camping trailers was deserted of all the people who, like us, had been enjoying an evening in front of a campfire. Abandoned pots and pans left out on the picnic tables confirmed the quick departures of others to their shelters, just as we had done. I pulled my head back inside and resigned myself to calling it a night.

Inside, I could smell the damp grasses, wet pine needles and the musty smells of my tent and sleeping bag. In the background, I caught the spicy aroma of the sage I'd brought back from gathering kindling the first night there. Pretty nice. Outside, rain sheeted down in violent, wind-driven gusts. The reality was, there was nothing to do but wait and see what the storm would bring. Heavy gusts bent my tent poles to a point where sometimes I was afraid they might not recover. The tent walls bellied inward as wind slammed against them, then mercifully, the poles would restore them to their original shape and I'd wait for the next onslaught. I wondered how Jeanine and Anne were doing.

I didn't have long to wait before finding out; a scream from one of the girls told me they were in trouble. I scrambled outside just as a flash of lightning lit up the area, making everything look like a grade-B suspense movie. Wind whipped the branches of the pines overhead and tore off sprigs of needles, sending them flying like miniature, tufted missiles. Icy rain plastered my shirt and shorts against my flesh.

A few yards away, Jeanine was crawling out of their tent entrance, followed by Anne. Their tent had collapsed, and to make matters worse had torn itself loose from the tent pegs they had pounded into the ground around its border. Obviously, a tent pole had collapsed under the pressure of the wind, weakening the entire structure. Now, their tent acted more like a lugsail, capturing the power of the wind, trying to break away from any would-be restraints. It wasn't something that could be fixed quickly, or in this downpour. Clearly, it wasn't going to provide shelter for the rest of the night.

"Get inside my tent," I yelled. "I'll do what I can here to keep yours from blowing away."

Anne hugged the tee shirt she had on as nightwear close around her, and shot a glance at my tent, still holding its own against the storm.

"Go," Jeanine yelled.

Anne hesitated. Another flash of lightning, followed by a crash of thunder near the edge of the campground, made up her mind for her. She staggered off, the rain pounding her hunched body with every step. I grabbed the door flap of their tent, now whipping violently in the storm, so I could see what needed saving inside. Jeanine thrust her head in beside me and yelled that all we needed were the sleeping bags. She had packed their food and suitcases in their car earlier. I grabbed the two bags, wadded them into a bundle, and shoved it into her arms. She stumbled off, huddling over the sleeping bags to shelter them from the rain as much as possible. Half way there, one of the bags belched outward from the loose bundle. She couldn't help but step on the trailing material, pinning it underfoot. The rest of the bag tumbled to the muddy, wet ground while the rain continued to pour down. She bent over, grabbed the now sodden bag, and managed the remaining distance to my tent.

I turned back to the task of securing their tent as best I could by yanking the poles free, and shoving the whole mess under the picnic table. I figured it wasn't so likely to blow away from there. Suddenly aware that I had given my tent up to the girls, I wondered what the hell I should do for shelter. Luckily,

Jeanine resolved the issue when she poked her head out of the vestibule and yelled at me to join them before I drowned. Dilemma solved—for the most part. I walked over and folded myself backwards into the vestibule.

Ordinarily, a tent vestibule is a handy add-on to provide the entrance with more protection and to offer a space to take off muddy boots. It doesn't have flooring, and isn't meant to be that much of a room, just an extended entryway. It didn't seem an appealing place to sleep, but it might have to do.

Jeanine handed me a wet towel and apologized for their having already used it in an attempt to get the worst of the water off themselves. I knelt in the vestibule and wiped off the excess water as best I could. Anne and Jeanine lay peeking out from under a sleeping bag. They had one bag, opened out flat on the tent floor, and another spread on top of themselves. The third was a soggy mess, and lay crumpled in the corner of the vestibule.

Europeans seem to have a very practical sense about nudity, and are not ashamed of their bodies. Wet as everyone was, it made sense to combine body heat to fight the cold that already had me shivering. I peeled out of my wet clothes and squirmed under the sleeping bag into the space they had reserved for me. I was immediately grateful for the warmth our contact provided.

CHAPTER TWENTY-SEVEN

IN THE MORNING, birds noisily chirped and flitted about the tree trunks and shrubbery looking for a meal as though the storm had been nothing more than a shower to settle the dust. The air was clear and sweet. Noises drifting around the campground indicated other people were up and about, restoring camp routines and offering more proof the storm was a thing of the past. I had squirmed into dry clothes, gathered up my wet stuff and given thought to throwing it in the dryer at the camp Laundromat. Instead, I headed for the bathrooms first, thinking there would be time to check out the dryer situation after taking care of necessities.

Later, when I got to the laundromat, Anne and Jeanine were sitting near the dryers reading magazines while the drums spun in slow, comforting rhythms. The warm air from the dryers felt good. I found a magazine and joined the girls to wait until a dryer opened up that I could use.

"Looks like we had the same idea. You beat me to it," I said.

Jeanine smiled at me. Anne kept her eyes on her magazine and said, "You know that saying you people have about early birds getting the worm."

I laughed. "Have you checked out your gear yet?"

Jeanine shook her head. "First things first. Right now, I don't even want to think about that damn tent."

"Can't say I blame you."

I told them I'd work on getting a fire going and make some coffee, if they were interested. They both assured me they thought the idea sounded wonderful. While the fire worked out whether it was going to smoke and go out, or dry out enough to get a good burn going, I pulled their tent and poles out from under the picnic table and unfolded the mess while trying not to get myself wet again. In terms of actual damage, things weren't so bad. They had one badly bent pole, that would probably have to be replaced, but the tent wasn't torn to shreds as I had feared it might be. I managed to bend the pole roughly into shape and reinforce it with a splint of kindling and duct tape. Always carry duct tape.

I gave the fire a little more attention and put a pot of water on for the coffee, then scrounged around and found the tent pegs, still embedded in the damp ground where the tent had torn loose. I set the tent back up so it too would have a chance to dry out. When I finished, I dumped some grinds into the steaming water for coffee. Nothing like strong cowboy coffee to get things going. Just in time, too, Jeanine and Anne were headed back from the Laundromat.

I poured them coffee, announced my plan for breakfast and made a quick trip to the camp store for a dozen eggs and a can of Spam. Behind the counter, Russell was panting so hard I had trouble understanding what he was trying to say, but no trouble interpreting the message over-all.

"Quite a storm," he said. "Couldn't ask for a better excuse."

"Excuse? Excuse for what?"

"I saw what happened to their tent last night."

I was unable to catch the next part of his jabber, but heard him say something about a "threesome".

"Nothing happened, Russ. Their tent blew down, we all got soaked trying to take care of it, and we did the best we could with my tent."

His face flushed, his eyes bulged, and I thought he was going to start dribbling down the sides of his mouth. "I'll bet you did. I'm sure you gave them your very best," he said.

"Just ring up the groceries, Russ. You're gonna give yourself a heart attack, you keep it up."

Back at the campsite, I sliced the Spam and let Jeanine fry it while I tackled the pancakes I had promised. We ate standing around the campfire. Anne and Jeanine were properly impressed with the pancakes, and dubious about the Spam. Nothing like camping to give you a great appetite and make you willing to try just about anything, though. They decided the Spam was not terrible, fried and eaten with eggs and sourdough pancakes.

"I'm sure our other visitors from Norway who are here on Harleys to ride Route 66 would be jealous of me right now," Jeanine said.

"I'm surprised that people from other countries even know about our Route 66."

"Oh, yes. You would be impressed by how many people dream to come here and rent a Harley Davidson motorcycle so they can actually ride on Route 66. Thousands. It's a very popular ambition for many people in Europe."

"So they ride in big groups, with a guide and a support van, and all that?"

"Yes, and I'm sure they eat well, but this is even better. I am confident of this. You are a good cook, Bobby," Jeanine said.

I soaked in the praise. "Thank you."

"But you have something going on in the back of your mind. Is it your investigation?"

"I guess you could say that. I still feel I need to figure things out about Daryl," I said.

"I'm sure you will do whatever you can to find out who did this awful thing, but you have to accept that you cannot always accomplish your goals, however worthy," Jeanine said. "And, you should remember, this is a real murder. Whoever did it is very dangerous."

I couldn't disagree with her, but I felt determined to do whatever I could. After cleanup, I put my cooking gear away and started up my bike. Anne and Jeanine were going to make a trip into town, hoping to find a replacement tent pole. I had decided to give the church another visit. Maybe I'd get lucky and find Amanda there. I wanted to ask her to go over whatever she could tell me about Daryl again, and decided I'd like to see what she would say about his claim that that's where Sheri had been murdered.

CHAPTER TWENTY-EIGHT

WHEN I GOT to the church, I heard faint sounds of organ music coming from inside. Could mean Amanda was there. That would be good luck, if it was her. I suppose Rudy, the mountain man from the rendez-vous, would say it was all a matter of destiny. Of course, it might not be Amanda playing the organ.

I waited until there was a pause in the sound and tried banging on the door at the side of the building. Nothing happened. So much for destiny. I went around to the front of the church and banged on the doors there. Same result. I went back to the side door and banged again.

"Mrs. Trainer, it's Bobby Navarro. We talked after church. Remember?"

I heard a chair, or bench, scrape against the floor.

"Mrs. Trainer?"

I heard the lock scrape as someone turned the deadbolt knob and eased the door open a little. I could barely see Amanda's face in the slim lighting. I gave her my most disarming smile.

"Hi. Sorry to disturb you. I was hoping we might talk again."

She flashed me an understanding smile and eased the door open a little further. "What would you like to talk about?"

I smiled and tried to look apologetic. "I'd like to talk some more about Daryl King."

She opened the door wider so I could come inside, then led me toward the organ. She sat on the bench and motioned me toward a chair close by.

"I keep getting mixed messages when I talk with him," I said.

Her smile told me, mine was not a unique experience.

I told her about my latest conversation with Daryl, about him saying Sheri had been murdered at the church.

"He said it happened here?" She stared at me with eyes wide and a horrified expression.

I nodded.

"He wouldn't tell me how he knew. When I asked him, he just got all funny again, but said I should talk to you. He claimed you would know about anything happing around the church."

"I can assure you, I don't know anything about that!"

I waited.

Her expression turned from looking puzzled to one of sadness. "I guess that's our Daryl for you."

I shrugged. "Yeah, I assumed if you heard or saw anything that would help the police solve a murder, you would have told them."

She looked past me. I couldn't tell if she was looking at something on the wall, or her gaze had gone elsewhere. "Well, of course," she said.

"I don't know where he gets some of the things he says, but I guess he believes they're all true. I suppose that's what counts most."

"I'm not sure it works that way for everything."

"Maybe Daryl has this confused," she said.

"Confused with what?"

"Poor little Betsy Horvath." She looked at me, all wide-eyed and puzzled at my not understanding, or knowing, what she was talking about.

"Sheri's death is not the first murder we've had occur in our little town. Betsy Horvath, a girl a little younger than Sheri, was murdered about... about two years ago. Betsy was part of our youth group too, just like Sheri."

I didn't tell her I knew about Betsy. I thought I'd get further if I let Amanda just tell her story.

"So you see, Daryl may have the two murders confused," she said.

"How could he do that?"

"Why does Daryl do anything?"

I grinned in understanding.

"And, while it happened two years ago, now with Sheri's death, it might seem to him like it just happened yesterday," she said.

"Daryl was awfully fond of Betsy. He had a very difficult time after her death."

"They were friends?" I said.

Amanda nodded slowly. "I'd say they were good friends, but not necessarily on the same wavelength. Daryl was quite taken by Betsy, smitten, people used to say. I don't think Betsy felt at all the same way about him. I think she cared about him—just in a different way."

There had to be nearly ten years difference in age between Daryl and the two girls who were killed. Awfully fond of her? I had to wonder about that.

"Was he stuck on Sheri, too?"

"That's hard to say."

She half-frowned and put her fingers to her mouth. "If you ask me, there are too many around here who find the younger girls attractive."

"Anyone in particular?"

I waited, hoping she might name names and elaborate. Instead, she flashed me a coquettish smile, as if to say she had caught herself saying something she shouldn't have.

"But, with Betsy, I think Daryl might not have even realized he had a crush on her. I think he tried telling himself he wanted to be like her big brother. He looked out for her, not that she needed protection."

"At some point she did. Someone killed her."

"Well, yes. Tragically, someone did."

"And Sheri?"

"Well, I think Daryl has tried to look after Sheri too. I don't think he had a crush on her, though, not the way he did with Betsy. "Sheri is nice... was nice... to Daryl. But, she was friendly with everyone. Maybe too friendly, sometimes."

"How so," I said.

"Well, Sheri liked to flirt, and she was a bit of a tease. I don't think she understood that you have to be a little careful who you flirt with."

"Did she flirt with Daryl?"

"A little. At times."

"Did he get any wrong ideas from that?" I asked.

She gave a little shudder. "Oh, I don't think so," she said. "I think it just embarrassed him a little, and made him feel protective of her."

She looked at me with round, thoughtful eyes.

I thought about Daryl taking on some kind of big brother role. I supposed it could have been like that. What did have me puzzled, was why Daryl had initially only talked to me about his buddy Ernesto getting thrown in jail—nothing about knowing, or being friends with either of the girls who were murdered. I'd have to give that more thought.

"So, as far as you know, Sheri could have been murdered here. Just like Daryl said."

"I suppose so."

"But, you didn't hear, or see, anything around the time it happened? I mean, if you were here. I guess you're saying you weren't, though."

"Oh, I was here, I'm sorry to say."

She tilted her head and pursed her lips in a look of grim determination. "And, I did see Sheri that morning."

"You did?"

She nodded with certainty. "I'm an early riser. I got here early, to get in some practice. I like doing that when others aren't so apt to be around. Since I'm not the regular organist, I don't always know the hymns as well as I'd like to. Of course... and this is something you shouldn't tell others... sometimes I just like to come here and use the organ to enjoy playing."

She raised her hand again to cover her face and stifle an embarrassed laugh. Then she fell silent. I waited. Her expression remained blank, then changed as though suddenly remembering what our conversation was all about.

"Sheri came by about the time I was finishing that morning. She said she was doing an errand for her mother. Beth, that's her mother, is active in the church too."

Amanda's face twisted into a quivering map of wrinkles and emotions. "Knowing what happened, I never should have left her there. But, there were others around. She wasn't alone."

"Then, you had no reason to think she was in any danger."

"I've tried to tell myself that, but we had already lost one young girl... I should have known better."

She reached for her purse and took out a handkerchief. I caught the smell of lilacs as she shook it loose, dabbed her eyes and blew her nose.

"Who else was around when you left?"

"Well, I think Daryl was working on something. And Deacon Thomas was here. Mike was here as well, and Gary too. But, I thought I heard someone leaving just before I did. I can't say who."

CHAPTER TWENTY-NINE

I DECIDED TO touch bases with Lucinda. I thought I needed to update her on my work. We met at the station, at one of the desks in the common area, where a number of officers were making phone calls, writing up notes and reports, or doing whatever it was their office work amounted to. Lucinda and I had poured ourselves coffee and were settled in at the desk she had used when I met her there before.

"So, your friend, Amanda Trainer, thinks Daryl may be confusing Sheri Norton's murder with Betsy Horvath's."

"That's what she said."

"And that's because he was so... taken with Betsy?" Lucinda said.

"Right."

Lucida sat there, tapping the eraser of a pencil on the desktop, frowning at the neat surface of the desk. I wondered what was going through her mind. After a couple of minutes, she stopped tapping and looked at me.

"What do you know about Betsy's case?" she asked.

"Pretty much just what you told me," I said.

"I told you her body was found in the woods, later stolen from the morgue and never recovered."

"Right," I said.

I started to take a sip of coffee, but stopped. "I don't see what you're getting at."

She cocked her head a little to the side. "I'm wondering what there is for Daryl to be confused about," she said.

I waited.

"Both girls were members of the same church, we know that much. So, both girls were known by a lot of the same people... exposed to the same people... I'll grant that much," Lucinda said.

Then, she looked at me with a piercing stare. "But we found one girl's body in the forest, and the other in the trunk of a car on the main street of town. Your buddy, Daryl, mentioned to you that Sheri Norton was killed at the church."

I felt the skin on the back of my neck prickle.

"Is he confusing the two murders because both girls were killed at the church?" Lucinda said.

She let her words sink in for a minute, looking at me thoughtfully. "And, if that's the case, how does Amanda Trainer know enough about it to say he may have the two girls confused?"

My ears were ringing. I still had that crawly feeling on my skin. I felt my pulse thumping an insistent beat in the veins of my neck. I didn't have an answer to Lucinda's question—except the obvious one. "What he told me, was that I should talk with Amanda some more, because she knows everything that happens there."

We both stared at each other in silence. After a time, Lucinda picked up her coffee mug, blew a soft breath across its surface, and then took a sip, cupping the mug in both hands. "I think someone from here needs to talk with Ms. Trainer about whatever it is she might know," she said. "The trouble is, I don't want to put too much heat on the church while you're there."

I felt as though I were somehow responsible for something I might not want to happen. Amanda had befriended me when Pastor Martin tried to drive me off. She had been nothing but kind and sweet to me. I didn't want to cause trouble for her, and somehow I felt having the police come down on her would be very upsetting. At some level, I knew it had to happen. At the same time, I felt I was betraying her if it did.

I shook my head, partly in disgust with my police work naiveté.

"I see your point," I said. "I should have thought of it."

"And done what?" Lucinda said.

"Asked her to explain what she meant."

"Don't beat yourself up so much. Again, you're coming up with very helpful information. You're doing great."

I drank some coffee and tuned in to the room surrounding me. The noises of phones and other conversations, an occasional scraping of furniture as someone adjusted their position, or got up for some reason, all melded into a background of sound and activity as before. The ringing in my ears had stopped, and my pulse seemed back to normal.

"So what now?" I asked.

"That's a good question," Lucinda said. "I'm giving that some thought. For now, I'm going to leave things as they are, and let you nose around. Meanwhile, what would you like me to tell you about Betsy Horvath?"

I explained to Lucinda that I had been wondering just how close Daryl and Betsy were before she was killed, and was curious as to what her parents may have thought about his hanging around. Had they reported him as a problem? Tried to get him to stay away? Anything to support the idea that he may have been stalking her?

Lucinda set her mug on the desktop and retrieved the pencil again. "When we talked with Mrs. Horvath about people Betsy saw a lot, she told us about Daryl being a friend... kind of a big brother figure. She didn't think it likely he would ever do anything to harm her. More likely, he would cause harm to anyone who threatened her in any way. Mrs. Horvath also felt Betsy was completely confident that she could control any situation involving Daryl. She had stood up for him anytime anyone suggested he might pose a problem. Of course... that might have simply made her all the more vulnerable."

"Especially if he thought there was something between the two of them she didn't share," I said.

Lucinda nodded. "Especially then."

"What about the guy who was arrested for Betsy's death?" I asked.

"Hispanic. Late twenties. A drifter. The kind of person you see going through just about any town in the Southwest. Not filthy, not especially clean, but homeless. Usually carrying a bedroll and backpack of his belongings. Sometimes looking for a ride, but also looking for a handout with a sign written on a piece of cardboard—out of work, trying to get to wherever.

"He was seen a couple of times hanging around near Betsy's school by others who knew her. Evidently, he managed to appeal to her good nature with his out-of-work routine. She actually gave him some money, probably her lunch money, according to her friends."

"Anything else tie him to the murder?" I asked.

Lucinda smiled. "A crucifix," she said.

I hadn't expected that for an answer. She went on to explain.

"When Betsy's body was found, she was nude, with clothes she had worn wrapped in a heap and dumped nearby. But a silver crucifix was found lying on her body. Her friends were able to identify it as looking like one worn by the drifter. Someone else saw a man fitting his description running through the woods near where the body was found.

"We put out an APB and he was picked up in Kingman. He admitted to owning the cross. He also admitted seeing the body, and running away, but said he didn't kill her or rape her."

"What about the cross?"

"That was the most unlikely part. He said he recognized Betsy when he saw her body, and felt badly for her because she had been nice to him. He said he took the cross off and laid it on her body as a token of his caring for her. He said he wanted to bless her soul to get into heaven, and that was the only thing he could think of doing. Then he tried running away because he figured we'd blame him for killing her."

She paused and took a big sip of coffee. "Needless to say, he got that part right," she said.

"Did Daryl fit into the picture in some way?" I asked.

Lucinda looked at me and smiled again. "He was with her when she gave the guy her lunch money. One of the friends later saw the two of them, Daryl and the

murderer, talking together downtown. Daryl admitted he gave the guy some money too. Denied they had
become best buds, or that they raped her together."

Chapter Thirty

THE SKY OVERHEAD shone clear and brilliant, another scorcher. A memorial service for Sheri Norton was going to take the place of the regular Sunday service. Lucinda was meeting me at the church. She wore a black dress. I guess you'd call it a business dress, on the conservative side and didn't show a lot of cleavage. She looked professional, young and pretty. Her hair tumbled down to her shoulders in soft waves. She had glossed her lips with a light color, making them look moist, but nothing to draw attention to anything other than her natural good looks. Her eyes were intelligent and engaging, but not with the underlying police attentiveness I had often seen before. Although, I noticed we both scanned the parking lot as we were going in.

Together, we walked inside without any great hurry. Mike caught my eye from the front of the church, where he was leading another couple to their pew. It was more than a passing glance, and certainly without any sign of friendly recognition. As Lucinda and I were about to slide into a vacant pew, I felt someone come up behind me and heard a muffled voice.

"Glad to see you made the service."

I turned around. It was Gary. I could smell his aftershave, something heavy and musky. He had on a grey, long-sleeved shirt and dark slacks. His head had the same reddish glow. It looked like he had gotten a fresh haircut. He reached around me and held out his arm, ushering us into the aisle as though he had selected it for our use.

"Poor kid, it's terrible that happened to her." he said.

I nodded to Gary as I slipped in behind Lucinda and sat down. He gave me a sticky smile, one that didn't seem quite right for the occasion.

Lucinda picked up a hymnal and thumbed to the first song. I decided to look on with her and not duplicate the whole routine myself. I felt the side of her body press lightly against me. The perfume she wore enveloped her hair like an ever so delicate halo of sweetness. I sensed her steady breathing and noticed tiny beads of perspiration on her brow and upper lip.

After a few minutes, the place had filled to capacity, and people were crowding at the back where there was standing room only. The Nortons, Sheri's parents, sat on the left in the pew closest to the front. They both looked grim, obviously struggling with the weight of their loss. They sat together, but seemed rigid, especially whenever their movements put them in touch with each other. A few people approached them close enough to lean over and offer quiet condolences, for which the Nortons appeared grateful.

Then Deacon Thomas came from the back area and started things rolling, the same way he would have on any other Sunday, except for a few differences. This time, he stammered as he spoke, and the grandiose air he projected the first time I saw him was missing.

The choir came on stage, along with Ben Edwards, the choir director. His face was calm, saddened by the occasion, but still reflecting the salesman's self-confidence. He led the congregation in a hymn that sounded very traditional, and pretty familiar. I recognized Teresa, the girl who liked my motorcycle. She looked uncomfortable as she stood at the far end of the line of singers. I assumed it was because she had been friends with the deceased murder victim.

Amanda was playing the organ. Ben gave her a quick, businesslike nod to signal the girls were ready. When the hymn was over, Pastor Martin announced the special purpose of the service. He seemed respectful and, like others, saddened by the events and the duty he had to perform for Sheri and her family. Nevertheless, he showed strength and determination to fulfill this function as leader of the flock. His sermon was simple, and seemed fitting for a young girl who was well-known and would be missed. There were no long eulogies or any of that fire and brimstone stuff. He acknowledged the tragedy of her passing, and the mystery of why things happen the way they do sometimes. He gave some words of hope and comfort, and then concluded with a suggestion to everyone.

"When a young girl dies," he said, "her soul goes straight to Paradise. Because her heart is pure. Let us pray to become like a young girl—pure in heart, pure in thought, and pure in all our deeds."

My stomach knotted up at the thought that whoever murdered her, or was in on it with Ernesto the cook, could still be sitting there with the rest of the congregation. I didn't feel comforted that thoughts of seeking purity would help much.

When the service ended, Gary and Mike began clearing the pews one-by-one. I turned around and noticed Daryl had come in and was sitting a few rows behind us. It was obvious he was having trouble keeping his emotions in check. He avoided eye contact with anyone, keeping his head down, except when he snorted in to overcome his runny nose. A thin, red line on his cheek showed where he probably had sliced himself shaving earlier in the morning. He was dressed for church, but the wrinkled white shirt, tie and what looked like a cast-off sports jacket, appeared totally out of place on him, and he looked uncomfortable wearing them. I don't think he noticed me at all.

When it became our turn to step into the aisle and join the movement toward the exit, Lucinda tugged lightly on my arm. I turned, and she leaned close so I could hear her lowered voice.

"See that man coming across the front? The one in the blue suit with the polka dot tie?"

I spotted the person she must be talking about. He was looking our way with a businesslike smile.

"That's Chief MacDonald, my boss."

The chief was a good sized man, in his middle forties, a bit burly. He had something of a paunch, but nothing major. He still had a full head of hair, dark, cut close, and wavy. His eyebrows were prominent and bushy. His face was stern, like he was used to giving orders, not taking them. His line merged with ours a little way in front of us. Chief MacDonald nodded at Lucinda. When he reached Pastor Martin, they exchanged a few words I couldn't hear. Then it was our turn with the pastor.

"Good morning, Bobby," Pastor Martin said.

I looked at him and shook hands, unsure of what to say. "That was an interesting meeting the other night—the Bible study group," I said.

He smiled with a brief lifting at the corners of his mouth, and turned his head toward the chief.

"This is the young man I mentioned to you," Pastor Martin said.

Then, Pastor Martin turned toward me. "Chief MacDonald also comes to our little Bible Study group, whenever he can," he said. "You might run into him sometime... if you continue to meet with us."

His tone suggested he didn't expect that I would. I glanced at the chief, frowning in my direction. Pastor Martin continued talking.

"Bobby—Mr. Navarro here—has been conducting his own investigation into our tragedy."

The Chief's face froze, his dark eyes forty-five caliber muzzles trained on the center of my forehead. He flashed a look at Lucinda, then back at me.

"How's that again?" the chief said.

"Apparently Mr. Navarro is concerned with whether you have the correct man in jail. He's conducting his own study of the matter."

The Chief drew himself a little straighter, although he clearly stood taller than me without the extra inch or two it gave him.

I shook my head. "Not really. I'm actually just here to visit the Canyon and enjoy the area a bit."

The Chief continued frowning in my direction.

"I happened to be the one who found Sheri's body," I said. "When I first came into town. That's why I'm here today. I've just felt caught up in her tragedy. I've had trouble getting her death out of my mind."

The Chief's gaze seemed to soften, as though with some understanding of what I might be talking about.

Pastor Martin stood, with a broad smile, waiting for whatever might come next.

Chief MacDonald half turned toward the pastor. "I don't believe we need any outside help," the Chief said.

He looked back at me. "I'm sure we can manage our affairs quite well without it."

"I have no problem with that," I said.

CHAPTER THIRTY-ONE

OUTSIDE THE CHURCH, I walked Lucinda to her Cherokee. She climbed in, and I shut the door for her. She started the engine and lowered the window. I could feel the built-up, superheated air escaping.

"Is there going to be a problem?" I said. "That thing with the Chief?"

"Oh, I already told you, I cleared your involvement with Detective Alvarez. I'm sure the Chief knows about you helping us out. He likes to stay on top of things, and murder is a very big thing in a town this size. I think he just had to put on a show for Pastor Martin without breaking your cover, not that you have much of a cover as confidential informants go."

"I was surprised to hear the Chief's a member of the Bible Study group. It's hard to picture him spouting Bible verses," I said.

She laughed and explained that he never did that sort of thing at work, at least.

"I know he plays poker with some of the boys once in a while, not that I'm supposed to know it. Maybe your Bible bangers have some other activities going on they haven't let you in on yet."

"I think that's a pretty safe bet," I said.

I watched her drive out, then went over to my bike, parked at the far end of the lot as usual. People were pouring out of the front of the church and heading downstairs for coffee and donuts. I didn't feel much like socializing, and had decided not to join them. I settled into my saddle and started the engine. Maybe a ride would be good.

I had my helmet on and the kickstand up, when I glanced back toward the church. Mike and Gary had hung back from the others, and stood talking to each other near the side exit. The door opened, and Teresa came out. She had traded her choir robe for a sun dress. Her hair was still in a ponytail. As she reached the bottom of the stairs, she headed across the parking lot, passing in front of the two goons. As she did, it looked as though Mike said something to her. Then his hand dropped to his groin, and he gave his crotch a couple of tugs and laughed.

I hit the engine kill switch and dropped the kickstand, jerking my helmet off at the same time. As I tossed the helmet over the sissy bar, I caught a glimpse of Daryl, nearer to the rear of the church. Apparently, he had noticed the incident as well. He looked upset, but frozen in place. I started forward. Teresa was closer to me now, walking hurriedly with the obvious purpose of putting distance between herself and the two goons.

"You okay?" I said when I reached her.

She managed a smile, and stopped.

I looked at Mike and Gary. They had seen me approach, and locked on me like gunnery radar. Their expressions hardened, but with a hint of pleasant expectation, either at the thought of what they might enjoy at Teresa's expense, or the thought of what they would enjoy doing if I interfered in her defense.

"They're so crude," Teresa said. "I can't stand them. They creep me out."

She shuddered quickly, then looked up at me. "Don't worry, I'm okay now," she said.

I studied her to make my own assessment. Her eyes were moist from tears trying to escape, but I couldn't say if it was from her encounter, or because of the memorial for Sheri. I guess she saw me take notice, because she shook her head, as if to say it was not because of Mike.

"I'm just upset because I feel so badly about Sheri," she said.

Mike and Gary suddenly shifted their attention toward Daryl, who quickly wheeled around and went toward the rear of the church. I wondered if he had his motorcycle parked in back. With a final glance toward Teresa and me, Mike and Gary strolled after the last of the congregation heading toward the basement where refreshments were being served. I looked down at Teresa.

"It's always harder when you lose someone close," I said. "Especially when you're both pretty young."

Teresa had dug a tissue out of her pocket and dabbed it against her eyes. "I knew someone who was killed in a car accident," she said. "A cousin of mine. But this is so much harder. It wasn't a freak thing that just happened. She was… raped. They raped her, and then they killed her."

Her mouth had shrunk into a hard line, the muscles in her face were taut. Her eyes glinted like chips of obsidian.

"They won't get away with it," I said. "I know that doesn't help much—it won't bring her back—but, they're going to be put away for what they did."

I realized we had both been saying "they", instead of "he", or "whoever it was".

"They?" I said.

Teresa jerked her head a little to the side and squinted toward the rear of the church, then she recovered and her eyes bore into mine.

"I think they're all responsible," she said. Her voice came out in a raspy, guttural surge. "It wasn't just...."

She cut her sentence off, clamping her lips without starting the next word. She gulped in a mouthful of air, and drew herself upright. "I'm sorry," she said. "I've got to go. I have to get home. My parents are expecting me."

CHAPTER THIRTY-TWO

JEANINE, ANNE AND I were planning to share a meal of flank steak, slow cooked in a gravy made with dried fruit, and accompanied by sauerkraut and potatoes. It was meant to be special. Jeanine apologized that it would take a little time. I said that was no problem and that I'd make a quick run to pick up some wine. I assured them I would be back in plenty of time for dinner.

I had spotted a liquor store I wanted to check out on the main drag. I drove down the one-way headed west, driving slowly enough I wouldn't go by it. When I passed Jack's Biker Tavern, I saw something that gave me a different idea. Not a very good one, as it turned out.

Mike's pickup was jammed into one of the few parking spots in front of the bar. Thinking about his harassment of Teresa earlier in the day, I wheeled in and parked my bike in the dirt at the edge of the parking area. I was also thinking about Amanda's comment that too many people were attracted to the younger members of the church and choir. Trouble was, I probably wasn't thinking enough.

Inside, I saw Mike at the far end of the bar, talking with a couple of guys I didn't recognize. He stood, leaning back with his elbows propped against the bar. I was sure he'd had a few, but he wasn't drunk. Not drunk enough to impair his strength or capability, at any rate. I know I shouldn't have gone in there looking for trouble, but sometimes you have to take the fight to the source of the problem.

"Mike!" I said, loud enough to overcome the volume of the jukebox belching out country music on the other side of the room.

He looked surprised, and then a little amused, as I walked up to his group.

"I thought, maybe I might buy you a beer, so we could talk," I said. "You know, talk about women. Well, for you, not really women I suppose, more like girls. You know, like Teresa at church. I guess you have a thing for the really young ones. The kind that are illegal." I said.

He lunged forward in a slight crouch, sending a wave of sweat, aftershave, and stale beer ahead of him. His left arm flicked out, and his thick fingers folded into a hard fist. It was a half feint, but would have staggered me if I had stayed in the way. I didn't.

I expected him to either head butt me, or go for the groin. He chose the groin. I rolled my hips and drove my arm down to block the blow, then pivoted back and slammed the heel of my hand upward, intending to catch him at the base of his nose. Instead, something exploded in the back of my head before my hand ever got near his face.

When I woke up, I was aware of being in a well-lit room, lying on something covered with crisp, clean sheets. My head rested on a thin pillow, and the slight move I made to explore my surroundings sent a searing spasm of pain throughout my skull, like a bullet ricocheting around the walls of a concrete bunker.

When I could hear again, and breathe a little, I opened my eyes. Someone wearing a uniform was standing over me. I guessed she might be a nurse.

"Welcome back to the land of the living," she said.

"I'm not so sure I'm ready for it."

She smiled. "Your head's going to be a little sensitive for a while," she said. "You've suffered a concussion."

My mind took me back to the scene inside the bar, where I had confronted Mike. Obviously, it hadn't turned out the way I had wanted.

"You took a nasty blow to the back of your head," the nurse said. "You're lucky your skull wasn't crushed.

I stared through my haze of semi consciousness, trying to make sense of where I was, what she was saying, and what must have happened. I thought of Mike's hands. They were gnarled and calloused, but I hadn't expected them to be hard enough to do that kind of damage, and I never had any sense of him throwing what would have had to be a hook to the back of my skull, either.

"How long have I been out?"

"Long enough. Right now, you just need to take things very easy. I'll let the doctor know you're awake."

She floated away from the bed, or gurney, or whatever I was on, and moved out of my range of vision. I knew better than to try to lift my head to follow her. After what seemed like a long several minutes, I heard quick, soft footfalls approaching. I opened my eyes, not having been aware of having closed them. The nurse's now-familiar face reappeared above me.

"It's okay for you to talk to him, but Doctor says you shouldn't take long," she said to someone who had entered with her. Then, she drew back again.

This time I chanced moving my eyes to follow her retreat, and to see who she had been talking to. I thought the movement would cause a load of pain. I wasn't disappointed. I winced until the throbbing ebbed a bit, then forced my eyes open again. A uniformed police officer stood beside my bed.

"You've been taken into police custody, Mr. Navarro," he said. "We're at General Hospital, and you're under the doctor's care for injuries sustained in the course of your alleged assault on someone in a local establishment."

He read me my rights, and then continued. "You won't be able to leave here until the doctor gives permission, and then we will take you to a secure facility until you can be arraigned. Do you understand what I've just told you, Mr. Navarro?"

I started to nod, but luckily stopped myself in time to avoid blowing my head off.

"I get the picture," I said.

The officer smiled and told me either he, or someone else, would be outside and that I should just try to lie there quietly.

CHAPTER THIRTY-THREE

SOMETIME LATER, I woke up again. I was able to flex my muscles and rotate my head enough to see that I was still in the hospital. I assumed the police were also still outside the closed door. I heard a low murmur of conversation, then the door opened and Lucinda entered the room.

I tried to smile. "Did I miss something? I wasn't expecting visitors."

"Not entirely a social call," she said.

"Sorry about that."

"Got yourself in a bit of trouble, didn't you?"

"Seems like it."

"Want to give me your version? I'm not here doing an investigation, and you don't have to tell me anything if you don't want to."

I shrugged under the sheet that was pulled up to cover my chest and shoulders.

"Don't have much to tell. One minute, I was downtown, talking with a goon from the church, and the next I woke up in here."

"You don't remember getting into a fight? Starting a fight, in fact?"

I hesitated. "We had a couple words. He made a move on me. I didn't even get in my first shot.

I tried to shift my position under the sheet a little. It seemed to work without my brains catching on fire. I decided that would have to do for progress.

"Like the saying goes, I never even saw it coming. I guess that old boy's faster than I thought," I said.

"You were hit from behind, in the back of the head by the bartender," she said. "He used a sap."

"That would explain things a little."

"He said you started a fight with one of his regulars. You remember anything like that happening?"

I grinned. "I went inside to tell Mike, from the church, that he should lay off the young girls there. I guess I've started feeling a little protective of one of the choir singers, Teresa Gonzales.

Suddenly I remembered dinner, the special dinner Jeanine and Anne were fixing for me. "Oh, Christ," I said. "What time is it? I'm supposed to have plans tonight."

Lucinda's mouth twisted into a sarcastic frown. "Afraid your plans have been canceled, Bobby. You're not going anywhere, on your own. Didn't they explain that to you?"

Outside, a siren wailed closer and closer to the hospital, then wound down as an ambulance approached the emergency entrance. I wondered if I had been treated to a similar bus ride earlier, but I had no memory of it. I could hear sounds in the hallway, the clanking of a cart or something, and the voices of staff going about the business of restoring bodies to a healthy state. I wondered how soon I'd hear my state of being was healthy enough to start the next round of this little episode.

"They explained I wouldn't be walking out on my own," I said. "Something about my starting a fight.

The way I remember it, Mike took a jab, tried to knee me, I tried to respond. Then, the lights went out. Technically, I think that should be self-defense."

She smiled. "The way they tell it, you came in looking for trouble, and the bartender had to step in to put a stop to it."

"He hit the wrong guy, as far as I'm concerned."

"All four of them tell pretty much the same story."

I stretched and moved my legs under the sheet again, feeling disgusted with myself for letting the whole thing happen. I should have known better than to go at him on his own turf.

"Actually, you may now have a friend you didn't know about." she continued. "As it turns out, there was one other witness. He won't stand up against Mike and his bunch face-to-face, but he spoke up about what happened, so I'm going to see if I can get you out of this."

I slowly turned toward her, ignoring the pain. She put her hand on my leg and gave it a little shake while perching on the edge of the bed.

"Daryl King came into the bar right behind you. He wouldn't talk to the police who showed up at the scene, but he called in and asked for me. I guess you're his new hero."

"Hero?"

"For standing up to Mike."

"I didn't even manage to hit him."

"Doesn't matter. As far as Daryl is concerned, you did something neither he, nor anyone else he knows, has had the *cahones* to try doing. You may just have made a breakthrough with our friend."

She gave my leg another little pat and told me to sit tight and not do anything that might upset the officer keeping watch on me. She said I might have to spend a few hours in custody, but she was pretty sure she could make the charge go away. She got up from the bed, wearing a big sister grin, and cupped her fingers in a little waving gesture.

"Oh, one more thing. About your dinner plans that got canceled—some very concerned person did some calling to find out why you never showed up when she expected you. She knows you were injured—not all the details—and she knows you're okay."

Lucinda turned and walked toward the door. "I'm sure you'll have a chance to make it up to her," she said.

CHAPTER THIRTY-FOUR

WHEN THEY RELEASED me the next day, both from the hospital and police custody, I bummed a ride from Lucinda to pick up my bike, then drove back to the campground, worried that Jeanine and Anne might have packed up and left by then. I could hardly blame them if they had. Planning on cooking a special dinner with their camp neighbor and finding out he's been arrested for getting involved in some barroom brawl didn't seem like the sort of thing to make them want to hang around.

I was relieved when I pulled into camp and saw their tent was still up in the site next to mine. Jeanine came rushing down from the camp store and threw her arms around me before I could drop the kick-stand.

"We've been so worried about you, Bobby," she said.

Anne was coming out of their tent. She started walking our way, a big, warm grin announcing her pleasure in seeing me.

"I'm really sorry I ruined dinner," I said.

Jeanine waved her hand across her face as if brushing away a bad odor. "Oh, that was nothing," she said. "We were just worried you had been hurt really bad. Well, I mean, worse than you were."

By this time, Anne had joined us. "When we realized something was making you very late, we started calling all over."

"Again, sorry about that," I said.

Jeanine shook her head. "Then we found out we were right, that you were in the hospital."

"Anybody tell you what happened?"

"They said you had been injured," Jeanine said. "I asked if you were in an automobile accident with your motorcycle. They wouldn't tell me exactly what happened, but they said it was not a... how did they say...? A vehicular accident. And, they said you were going to be all right."

Anne broke in to finish the statement, "But they said you wouldn't be released right then. That was really all they would tell us."

Both women stood close, looking up at me, waiting for me to fill them in. I hated having to tell them how I came to be, not only in the hospital, but under police guard.

"I got knocked out with a sap, a weapon filled with lead," I said.

Their eyes widened in unison. I heard the intake of air as they gasped. I shook my head to let them know it wasn't a huge deal.

"How did that happen?" Jeanine managed to say.

I explained about going into the bar where I saw Mike's pickup truck parked, and gave them a short account of why, and what took place, and the fact Daryl stood up for me with Lucinda.

"Isn't that the person you told us about? The person who told you he knew something about that girl's murder?" Jeanine asked.

"That's the man," I said. "I was lucky he showed up. And lucky he was willing to talk to Lucinda. Tell her what happened. Otherwise I'd still be in jail."

They asked if I had eaten, and I said I had, but the little bit of food on my hospital tray hardly counted as a meal. Anne suggested we all go into town and offered to drive us all in their rental car.

"Let me see what I can come up with for a change of clothes, and give me a few minutes to shower and run a razor over my face," I said.

We ended up eating Mexican food at a place on the western end of the strip along Old Route 66. It gave us a chance to play more catch-up. The girls were more convinced than ever that I was heroic for confronting Mike in behalf of the young girls at the church. They were also critical of me for going into the bar to take him on, and for taking my concerns up with Mike, rather than the police. I did my best to convince them that this really wasn't the Old West, full of lawlessness and killers, and that I hadn't been taken down by an outlaw gang.

"So, I'm confused," Anne said. "You have been helping the police try to determine whether this Daryl person knows who committed murder, while they think he might have been the one who did it, himself. But, it was Daryl talking to the police that kept you from having to go to jail for your fight with Mike."

"That's about it."

"And, normally, this Daryl, won't talk to the police, or nearly anyone else, but on this occasion he did. He told them the fight was not all your fault, and the police believed him this time."

I nodded my head.

"I think it's all very confusing," Anne said.

I grinned at her. "I can't argue with that."

CHAPTER THIRTY-FIVE

I WAS SUPPOSED to take it easy for a few days, but I wanted to thank Daryl for standing up for me. Mondays were normally his regular days for tending the grounds at the church, I had learned, and I found him taking care of the rose bushes that bordered the parking lot. He was kneeling with a container of gardening tools and supplies. He had his Tee-shirt off and tucked into his waistband so it hung down behind him like a breechclout. His skin was burnt brown and glistened with sweat.

I watched as he went over each plant, plucking a bug from time to time and dropping it into a bottle of liquid. Kerosene, was my guess. Japanese beetles can be a real problem for roses. My landlady in New York has lots of roses, so I knew about that.

Once each plant was rid of pests, he picked up a cardboard tube of powder and dusted it, then leaned back, arms at his sides, looking the whole plant over, like a mother inspecting a little kid before sending it off to school.

As I walked toward him, Daryl remained absorbed in tending the roses. I got close enough that I thought I'd better let him know I was there.

"Shit, man. You scared the hell out of me," he said. He wiped his hands on his jeans and stood up, grinning like I was a long lost friend.

"I just wanted to say thanks for telling the police my side of what happened at the bar," I said.

He looked embarrassed.

"I know you don't like sticking your neck out with the police," I said. "And I wouldn't blame you for not wanting to get on Mike's bad side, either."

He shook his head. "Mike don't scare me," he said. But he didn't look at all convincing, and I remembered the way he stood, wavering, at the church when Mike made the obscene gesture at Teresa.

I saw Daryl's motorcycle, parked just around the back of the church, and asked him if he'd like to take a ride. He accepted the invitation without hesitating.

"Hey, where the hell do you live?" I said. "I would have asked you if you wanted to go for a ride before, but I had no way of getting ahold of you."

He laughed and told me he'd have to run by his place before we took off on our ride, and I could follow him there. He said he didn't have any phone at the minute, because he got cancelled when he couldn't pay his bill. "Just as well," he said. "I don't want anybody calling me anyway."

When Daryl finished his gardening chores, he put his supplies away, climbed on his bike and led the way to his place. It was little more than a rented room in a seedy part of town. There was a tiny apartment stove and a small sink, side-by-side. Two cabinets hung on the wall above the sink, and a small refrigerator was crammed into the space opposite the sink and stove. Not much to call home, but I was surprised at how neat and tidy everything was. No dirty dishes in the sink, or food-crusted pots on top of the stove. The single bed was neatly made, with a sheet and Army blanket tucked under the mattress and pillow at one end. A tiny dresser sat next to the bed, with an alarm clock on it, and another dresser sat at the other end of the room with a television perched on top. I didn't check out the bathroom, but I had the feeling it would be clean and neat too.

Daryl rummaged through the top drawer of the dresser and dug out some money from a stash he apparently kept there, grabbed a leather jacket and said he was ready, unless I wanted a beer first. I told him I could wait. We picked up I-40 and headed west for a few miles, then turned south on Highway 89. The highway went through the Prescott National Forest, and offered enough beauty to take my mind off murder and rape and just about everything else. Daryl stayed in my rearview mirror, close enough for us to clearly be riding together, but not right on my rear end. I appreciated that. Some people lag behind too far, and others act like they want to run you over.

Before reaching the town of Prescott, the road branched off into 89A, which took us to Jerome instead. Jerome is an old mining town clinging to the steep mountainside. It's picturesque to say the least. I love it. I made my first visit there when properties for sale could be found well under fifty thousand. It was tempting at the time. I should have bought. Now, Jerome's been discovered and prices have gone way up. A lot of the old buildings in the commercial area have been developed into tourist shops selling anything from kaleidoscopes and dream catchers to real estate. Some of the people who have moved in are artists. Some just have an artistic sense with their renovation. In any case, things looked good. Since those old places needed a wealth of TLC, it's good to know the decay has been checked and that Jerome is now an active community.

We parked our bikes and left them in the public parking lot at the lower end of town, accepting the idea that Jerome is best seen by foot. We found a restaurant where we could order beer and something to eat. My stomach was growling, and I assumed from watching him at the diner that Daryl was always ready to eat. A girl in a black skirt and flowery top greeted us and gave us a seat next to one of the large, plate glass windows facing the sidewalk. She took our orders for drinks and said our waiter would be right out.

When our waiter came along, he had our beer and two glasses of water. I ordered a chicken sandwich. Daryl went for barbecue pork on a bun. So often when I eat somewhere, I spend the whole time people-watching, because I'm usually by myself. Trouble is, when I'm not by myself I have trouble figuring out what to say. That didn't prove to be the case with Daryl, at least not this time. It was as though we had a lot of catching up to do. We talked about riding, and rides we had taken. Daryl had been to Jerome and Prescott numerous times, and had even visited Montezuma's Castle, all attractions in the area I was familiar with. There was none of the fidgetiness about him I had seen at the diner. He had become a different person.

When our food came, we dug in, but at a more leisurely pace than I remembered seeing Daryl eat before. At some point I was distracted by a trio of people walking by on the sidewalk outside our window. They were trying to peer inside. I guess they wanted to see if it looked crowded. Their expressions said they were starving. I suppose I would have felt guilty taking our time if the place had been jammed full. I'm a sucker for a hungry face. Fortunately, I didn't need to worry, or hurry, and our waiter wasn't trying to hustle us along either.

"So, tell me," I said. "What's with that bunch at the Bible Study?"

Daryl shrugged. "They like hanging out," he said.

He eyed me warily, then seemed to remember that our relationship had changed. He rested his elbows on the tabletop, cupping his hands together. "They have a poker game once a week," he said.

"It didn't look like poker when I was there."

He grinned a little. "The poker game is on a different night. They have to get to know you before they'll let you in on that."

I nodded. "How about Mike and Gary? They're not typical church members. They act more like bodyguards. Or a goon squad."

Daryl laughed, then wiped his mouth with a napkin, wading it up afterward and setting it in a rumpled ball beside his plate. "Well, I wouldn't call them 'typical' churchgoers, exactly. Gary takes it seriously. Mike is Mike. They all knew each other long before they came here," Daryl said. "They did time together in the same prison."

Daryl explained that Pastor Martin and his two sidekicks had all been in a motorcycle gang, somewhere in the Midwest. I knew they had ridden together, from Gary's comment after the Bible study meeting, but I didn't know it was in a gang, or club.

Daryl went on to explain Pastor Martin, Gary and Mike got busted on some drug dealing charges, along with felony assault, and ended up doing five-to-ten in prison. Pastor Martin figured out that he'd do better by 'finding God' than he would standing up to a hard-core bunch of inmates from a rival gang. Gary went along with the program, and actually got hooked. Mike was pretty much the same then as now, handy for Pastor Martin to have in his corner but by no means hooked on anything but his own capability for violence.

"So, Pastor Martin used to ride wearing a set of colors," I said.

Daryl smiled again. "Leader of the pack."

"Well, I'll be damned."

Our waiter came by and asked if we wanted another beer. I swallowed the last bit in my bottle and handed the empty to him with an affirmative nod. He soon returned with two chilled bottles, put bar napkins down to absorb the moisture and set them on the table. I raised my bottle and clinked it against Daryl's, then took a swallow.

"Then you showed up, and started asking too many questions," Daryl said. "That presented a problem."

I shrugged. "It's what I do," I said.

We sat quietly for a while again. Finally I broke the silence.

"So, how about you?"

Daryl shook his head. "People at church either have to fit in, or move on. I don't fit in exactly, but I'm no threat as far as they're concerned either. My half-brother, Ben, and Pastor Martin get along real well. I do handiwork around the place, so they don't mind me."

His expression hardened. "As long as I remember my place," he said.

Then he looked up and grinned. "Pastor Martin gets pretty much everything he wants from the church. As long as nobody comes along and makes problems."

"Like me."

"Like you."

"So, why don't you tell me what you know about the murder, and I can get the hell out of everybody's way?"

CHAPTER THIRTY-SIX

DARYL STARED ACROSS the table at me for a long minute without speaking, then slowly nodded his head as though acknowledging the time for him to speak up had come.

"Two separate girls, both murdered, both raped," he said.

I picked up my beer and took a swallow, then settled in to hear what he would say, now that he was finally going to tell me what happened.

"You found Sheri's body in Ernesto's car trunk," he said.

I nodded.

"Ernesto was with me the day it all happened," Daryl said. "He had just gotten the car, and was all excited—you know? Like, I don't think he had ever owned a car before. He knew how to drive, but that was about it. He was at church, helping me finish up some stuff I was working on, so he could take me out for a demo ride."

"Okay...," I said. I took another sip of beer.

Daryl leaned a little closer across the table. "When we went outside, the car wasn't there. We assumed somebody was playing joke on him, but after a while I got a bad feeling. A joke is a joke, right? But you don't keep the dude's car too long."

I agreed.

"I finally dropped him off at work... at the restaurant... and said I'd help him report it to the police later. Only, later the police got to us, both of us. When I found out Sheri's body had been found in Ernesto's car, I couldn't believe what was happening."

He studied me for a couple of minutes and then continued. "Another girl dead. The cops said she was found in Ernesto's car. I told them someone had stolen it. They thought we were both lying, and they stuck Ernesto in jail. All they were after, was to grab somebody they could hang this thing on, same as before. Like I told you."

"Like before," I said.

"Couple of years ago, girl by the name of Betsy Horvath was killed. Same thing. Police arrested a guy, a Mexican, and stuck him in prison."

"They questioned you about that first one, too, didn't they?" I asked.

"Yeah, they talked to a bunch of people, as near as I could find out. They wanted to blame me... because Betsy and I were friends." His mouth grew taut, his eyes squinted nearly shut.

"They knew we were close, so that made me a suspect. That... and the way they chose to take some of the things I tried telling them."

"Oh?" I said.

He gave me a quick, appraising glance.

"Betsy was just about the sweetest thing you could ever hope to know," he said. "I don't mean like, hot or sexy. I mean deep down. She was just a real sweet kid. I tried telling them that."

His voice trailed off. He stared at the table for a few seconds. "I really cared for her a lot," he said. "As a person. She was like a little sister to me. I tried to look out for her. "

"And they got the wrong guy for her death?" I said.

"Damned right they got the wrong guy."

Daryl's face grew contorted with some deep, inner fury. "I tried to tell them what had happened, what I knew, but that just convinced them all the more I had something to do with killing her."

His eyes bore into mine, commanding my attention with a vice grip of anger, daring me to question his declaration. "I know, because I helped steel her body," he said.

When I got past my surprise enough to talk in a reasonably calm voice, I asked Daryl why he had stolen Betsy's body, and who he had helped to do it.

"My half-brother Ben said we had to get her body away from the police before they could do all their examination stuff. He made me go along with him. That's how I know Ben was the one who did it. We buried her body in the woods, in a place we knew nobody would ever find her."

I had been holding my breath, without realizing it, while Daryl poured out his confession regarding taking the body of Betsy Horvath. I let it out as quietly as I could, and drew in another, not sure what to say. Daryl waited several moments, perhaps wanting to see what, if any, response I would make. Then, he continued.

"For a while, the police thought I was the one who killed her, and that I was trying to blame Ben for it to get out of trouble."

He shook his head. "I was in trouble a few times when I was a kid. Sometimes it was for something I had done, and sometimes I was just the one who got blamed for stuff that happened. People always believed anything Ben told them, and always thought I was lying to cover up. I told the police Ben must have been the one to kill Betsy, but they said I was lying to protect my own ass. I kind of freaked out, and they ended up not believing me about anything, except I must have been involved in killing her. In the end, they let me go anyway. In the meantime, they picked up this other guy who'd been hanging around. Some of Betsy's friends remembered seeing him the day she was killed."

"You and Ben took Betsy's body, and buried it somewhere?"

He nodded.

"Didn't you tell the police you could show them where her body was? They'd have to look, at least."

He shook his head, his mouth quivered, his nose was runny and tears coursed down his face. "They told me what would happen to me if I did that," he said.

"The police told you.?"

He shook his head. "Mike and Ben," Daryl said. "They made it clear I had to keep my mouth shut to the police, and forget anything ever happened. If I did, they said everything would straighten out. If I didn't, they said I would end up in the ground, keeping Betsy company."

CHAPTER THIRTY-SEVEN

AFTER OUR LUNCH, and Daryl's revelations, we walked back down the hill to the public parking lot, where we had left our bikes. I don't think we said one word on the way. I barely noticed any of the buildings we passed this time, even those for sale or under refurbishment. Normally I would have been looking them over, filling my head with images of what it might be like to be living there, becoming part of a community. Not this time. When we got to our bikes, I grabbed my helmet and climbed on mine, then sat there without putting the helmet on.

"So, you figure your half-brother, Ben, was responsible for killing both girls," I said.

He just looked at me, in silence.

"Did you have anything to do with putting Sheri's body in the car, or driving it to where I found it later?" I said.

He shook his head. "Nothing," he said. "I figure Ben and Mike must have taken care of it on their own this time."

I thought about his answer.

"Mike takes charge whenever shit needs to be cleaned up," Daryl said.

"Did they say anything about it to you?" I asked.

"Yeah. They told me to keep my mouth shut again. Like the last time," he said. "They knew I cared about both girls, Betsy most of all. All Mike ever wanted, was getting in the girls' pants. Age doesn't matter, with them. They want you to think they're God-fearing, good people all the time, then they try to score on young girls. Not just Mike. Others too, including Ben. Pastor Martin has to know what's going on with them, but he lets them get away with it. I don't know how they do that. One thing for sure, though, when Mike tells you to keep your mouth shut, you know he means it."

Daryl absentmindedly scuffed the toe of his boot on the pavement. "They were afraid I might spill something to the police. Believe me, I wanted to. I tried to. Like I said, Betsy and I were really close, and Sheri was good kid. I have trouble with the police, though, and they still want to hang something on me. They think I helped kill Betsy."

"So, this was never just about you thinking Ernesto was innocent. It was about what happened to the girls."

He nodded his head in slow emphasis. "Yeah. I mean, Ernesto shouldn't hang for what happened to Sheri, and neither should that other dude for what happened to Betsy. But, mainly I feel bad about what happened to the girls."

"Why did you act like you barely knew them when we first talked?"

He shrugged. "What would have been going through your head if I said I was friends with Sheri, or if I said the same thing about Betsy?"

I started to flip out an answer, but it got stuck in my throat. To be honest, I was thinking I would have figured he was a guilty pervert, but I didn't want to admit it to him.

He nodded and twisted his mouth into a sarcastic grin. "That's what I thought," he said.

He lifted his leg over his bike and sat down. "And, you would have put me right at the head of your suspect list. Especially when you started hearing some of the things people always go around saying about me."

"Just to be upfront, I still don't know for sure where to put you on my list, or what list I should have you on," I said.

He nodded, as though my statement was something he expected. Then suddenly I understood why he had been happy to have me talking with Amanda. She had already sorted out those things out for herself. I might listen to her, and I had.

"People always believe Ben, before they believe me," he said.

"You know, I talked with Ben recently," I said.

I shook my head, wondering where I was going with that thought, what its relevance was to Daryl's confession.

Daryl put his helmet on and fastened the chinstrap.

"He told me a lot of stories about you two as kids," I said. "About those things you got in trouble for."

Daryl shrugged and turned his head toward me. "I did my share of stuff I shouldn't have, but I didn't do most of the things Ben, or others, claimed I did."

"You didn't kill the rats and hang their bodies on the schoolyard fence for a Halloween prank? How about that girl you got in trouble over?"

"I never did hurt any rats, and the thing with that girl wasn't the way everybody wanted to believe. Anyway, I was a kid then. I'll bet you did some things when you were a kid."

"Ben said you tell things that you want people to believe, maybe the way you wish they happened as well, but not necessarily the way they did happen."

Daryl's eyes hardened and his jaw muscles stood taut. "Maybe I'm not the only one who should be accused of that. I guess you have to choose who to believe for yourself. You been after me to explain how I knew Ernesto is innocent—now I've told you."

I went through the motions of starting the engine and leaning against the weight of my bike to stand it upright and take it off the kickstand, but was only half aware of the rumble and vibration. I heard Daryl start his. I eased out of the parking lot with Daryl close behind me, and retraced our ride down the mountain toward Prescott, then north on eighty-nine to pick up US 40 and back to Williams.

Some of the ride was heavy scented with the smell of bark and pine needles that had been roasting in the sun all day, but I barely noticed. Some of the ride offered distant views of hills turning shadowed and purplish as the afternoon sun dropped behind the high range ahead of us. Some of it bordered open country where Herford cattle compete with deer and elk for forage. Throughout the ride, the steady cadence of our engines and exhaust rolled out what would normally be a soul-soothing concerto of road music. All I could hear on this ride, was Ben's voice telling me I couldn't believe everything Daryl said, and Daryl pointing out he had told me what I had been after him to find out.

When we got to Williams, the sky behind us was tinted pink, the air had chilled, and traffic patterns both on Interstate 40 and the access road into town attested to people's eagerness to reach their various destinations for the evening. I pulled over and stopped on the shoulder. Daryl came up alongside me.

"Thanks again for telling me. I know it had to be hard for you to talk about all that," I said.

He shrugged and nodded his head. I kept talking.

"And, I can understand why you figured the police wouldn't listen—same old-same old—and you'd end up taking the fall for it."

I wanted to tell him I believed him over whatever Ben would claim. I didn't, though; I was still sorting that one out.

"I'll see you around," I said.

He lifted his hand in a two-finger salute and drove off. I released the clutch handle, pulled back onto the access road and headed toward the campground, trying to sort through my muddle of thoughts, while a chilling realization of the danger Daryl had put himself in by talking with me grew larger in the pit of my stomach. I had no doubts in my mind about Mike. He meant it when he told Daryl to keep his mouth shut, and now I had stirred up a huge nest of fire ants by poking around the church and asking questions—and getting Daryl to open up to me.

CHAPTER THIRTY-EIGHT

I MADE MY way to the campground, and was glad to see Jeanine and Anne there. Part of me needed space to think, but the other part wanted to be assured the people I had come to know, even a little, were okay. It wasn't just Daryl I had put at risk by poking around, it was anyone, and possibly everyone, I had talked with. If Mike was the cleanup guy, I felt sure he would have no problems going however far he needed to put a lid on the pot I had stirred up. That would include Jeanine and Anne.

"Hi, Bobby," Jeanine said as soon as I turned off the ignition and dropped the kickstand. "It was a beautiful day for you to be out on your motorcycle. Did you have a nice ride? You look so serious."

I tried to give her an I'm-feeling-good smile. I think I managed more of a glad-to-see-you smile, or maybe simply a smile of appreciation, for her greeting.

"It was a good ride," I said. "We went to Jerome. Have you ever been there?"

She said they had not, and I explained its history as an old mining town, now attracting artists and tourists. Then I told her I had ridden there with Daryl.

Her face lit up. "Oh, that's good," she said. "I should think that must have given you more opportunity to become closer with him, and learn what he can tell you about the murder."

I smiled at her enthusiasm, but now had concerns about my talking with her and Anne.

"It did that," I said.

I stretched, and discovered how tight my neck muscles had become, then shrugged out of my leather jacket, slinging it across the seat of my bike, and walked over to the picnic table. Anne handed me a bottle of beer without my even asking. Sometimes it's pretty nice being looked after. I wasn't sure I deserved it.

"Would you like to join us for dinner?" Anne said. "You can tell us all about Jerome, and your ride."

"I'd love to share dinner," I said. "But, I need to touch bases with Lucinda, Officer Diaz, the police-woman I've been working with. Daryl finally opened up a little and talked to me. I need to let her know what he had to say."

I took a pull on my beer while digging my cell phone out to call Lucinda, then sat on the end of the picnic table with my feet resting on the bench seat. The phone rang several times, then went to her message box. I left Lucinda a brief heads-up about my talking with Daryl and asked her to call me back.

While the girls prepared dinner, I sipped my beer and shared some of my talk with Daryl. I told them about Pastor Martin's background and his setup at the church, explaining that Pastor Martin had gotten religion in prison, stepped out a free man and managed to set up his own church. Next thing that happened, he found himself a reputable member of the community.

That had its advantages, I explained, both for Pastor Martin and his closer followers, like his two bodyguards. Unlike a lot of ex-cons, Pastor Martin was now assumed to be on legitimate business, no matter what, no matter when, no matter where. Even if he should be stopped while driving with alcohol on his breath, he'd likely be given a break rather than a sobriety test, if he wasn't too drunk. It also made all the difference if Mike roughed up someone who had met with Pastor Martin's disapproval. After all, it was the word of a local pastor versus someone being accused of trying to make trouble.

The church also gave Pastor Martin a decent income, something not always available to an ex-con just out of prison, and no one questioned its legitimacy. I'd have to say though, to his credit, Pastor Martin hadn't shown noticeable signs of greediness. He dressed well, but not too lavishly. A nice watch, but not a Rolex. Shoes in nice shape, but something available in any department store. And, his car was a late model used car he probably had gotten at Ben's Autos.

No one questioned Pastor Martin's behavior or intentions when it came to his female parishioners, either. Daryl claimed Pastor Martin had an appetite for the ladies, which he indulged in his office, at home, or anyplace else. That went for the married ones, as well as the singles. For an ex-con, he had it made. And his followers had it almost as good.

"Why does everyone in the church put up with this Pastor Martin and his cronies, especially when young girls are involved," Anne said.

"Well, in Daryl's opinion, the members of the congregation have either been turning a blind eye, or decided to find another church after a brief discussion with Pastor Martin's two bodyguards."

"What does that mean, 'blind eye'?" Anne said.

"They didn't see anything going on because they didn't want to see anything going on."

"This Pastor Martin sounds like a horrible person," Jeanine said.

"Well, evidently Pastor Martin has always been there when a member of the congregation became sick, needed counseling, or help managing the loss of a loved one—just like a pastor is supposed to be," I said.

"And, as for the congregation, I'm sure some of them are good people, and some not so good. Over all, they are happy to be members of the flock. Happy to come together. Happy with life. Of course, two of their younger members, Betsy Horvath and Sheri Norton, aren't part of all that happiness anymore, and I have to believe Teresa, and others, are in danger of losing their happiness sometime in the future."

"I am not a religious person," Jeanine said. "And, what you are telling us, gives me more reason not to change."

I had to laugh and admit I shared her view of Pastor Martin's Holiness Pentecostal Church of the Brethren.

Anne interrupted her cooking long enough to pour herself a glass of wine and offer me another beer. I had barely gotten a thankyou out of my mouth when my phone rang. It was Lucinda.

"Thanks for getting back to me," I said. "I have some news for you."

CHAPTER THIRTY-NINE

I GAVE LUCINDA a quick rundown of my meeting with Daryl.

"He says he had nothing to do with either murder, but admits helping his half-brother, Ben, steal the body to hide evidence," I said. "Taking Betsy Horvath's body was all Ben's idea, according to Daryl. That's why he believes Ben either raped and killed her, or was a part of it. He thinks Ben is guilty of killing Sheri Norton, because of what Ben did to cover Betsy's murder—you know, stealing her body. That's why Daryl has been saying it's the same as last time."

There was a long silence on Lucinda's end of the line. Then, she suggested I come to her place and fill her in more. I told her we were just about to eat dinner, and agreed to meet her at her place afterward.

Lucinda's home was in a nice neighborhood with stucco houses, Spanish architecture, and small but neat yards. When I pushed the button for the doorbell, I heard Miguella's voice on the other side calling out to her mom that I was there. She threw open the door with a big grin, and a tiny voice.

"Hi," she said. Her voice sounded excited, as though I had come to a party just for her. She was wearing a white dress with ruffles that made the bottom stand out, like the kind of dress I imagined a young princess might wear. Her hair was tied with a blue ribbon made into a bow on the side of her forehead.

"Hi, Miguella. You sure look pretty today."

She smiled and pulled the hem of her dress out a little to show it off. "Thank you," she said.

I caught a glimpse of Lucinda in the kitchen, off the living room.

"Invite our guest to come inside, *Mija*, don't make him stand outside where it's hot."

I took the hand Miguella offered me. It was small, moist and warm, and I felt honored that she gave me her hand to hold. Miguella pulled the door open wide and I stepped inside, feeling like I should be careful not to step on her in the process. I guess I felt overly conscious of a need to be on best behavior. Miguella led me toward the kitchen.

"Something smells good," I said

"We had lasagna. Miguella's favorite," Lucinda said.

"Mine too," I said.

"We were just cleaning up," she said.

Lucinda was wearing a turquoise skirt, with a white blouse. Her hair was down, held off her forehead with a blue headband. Her smile was brilliant, and her face seemed to glow. She motioned toward a bottle of Chianti sitting on the counter next to a corkscrew. "Why don't you go ahead and open it," she said. "There's another wineglass in the cupboard. We can have a glass while you tell me all your news."

I took down a glass, opened the wine, and poured. I waited while she finished putting what looked like a pan of brownies into the oven, then handed her a glass and touched it with mine.

"To home-cooking. Always the best," I said.

She smiled. "Do you cook?"

"Actually, I do."

Her expression said she was a little surprised, but liked the idea. She led the way out onto a patio at the rear of the house, off the kitchen.

"What kind of cooking do you do?" she asked.

"Pretty much anything. I guess you could say, I grew up in the kitchen. My ma wasn't all that great a cook. My old man treated her really nasty when he didn't like something, which was most of the time. Her solution was to drink more and cook less. I kind of took over to avoid the bad scenes."

"I never knew that, back in high school. That's terrible. But, I'll bet you became a good cook."

"Not the worst, but I can't say how good either."

She smiled and took another sip of her wine.

"Sweetie, why don't you help Mommy by putting away the silverware like I showed you? Bobby and I are going to sit here on the patio and talk some business while the brownies bake."

Miguella grabbed a towel and began drying and putting away silverware, throwing a quick backward glance toward us as though checking to make sure we were settling down to business.

A thought flashed though mind, wondering how often Lucinda worried whether something might happen to Miguella if anyone decided to play rough in an attempt to discourage her from investigating a particular crime. I took a quick sip of wine and launched into my update.

"Now I understand why Daryl was going on about this murder being the same as last time," I said. "It wasn't just because Ernesto is Hispanic and so is the guy doing time for Betsy Horvath's murder. It's because he thinks his half-brother, Ben, is the murderer in both cases.

"Really?"

"It's what he told me. When Betsy was killed, Ben made Daryl help him steal her body from the morgue to prevent forensic analysis. Ben and Pastor Martin's bodyguard, Mike, told Daryl to keep his mouth shut—in both cases."

Lucinda sat in silence for a minute. "And, he denies having anything to do with their rapes and murders?"

"Right."

She shook her head and pursed her lips in a way suggesting she wasn't buying Daryl's story yet.

"Daryl has a history of denial and finger pointing to protect his own hide," she said.

I shrugged. "He said he didn't think the police would believe him. Said he tried to tell what happened at the time of Betsy's death, and nobody believed him."

"How much does Mike fit in, according to Daryl?" Lucinda asked.

"According to him, Mike's the clean-up guy. Whenever there is any problem that might affect Pastor Martin's Holiness Pentecostal Church of the Brethren, Mike takes care of it. That goes for anything from keeping people in line to making any kind of problem that does occur go away. Gary helps Mike out. They were all in prison together, and rode in the same biker club before that."

Lucinda took a sip of her wine and stared off to the side with a speculative expression in her eyes. I let her mull things over for a minute before saying anything else.

"It could make some of Daryl's tongue-tied behavior, or refusal to talk at all, more understandable," she said. "Pretty reasonable, if he's been telling the truth."

"It's a tough one," I said. "I talked with Ben, and he told me about things Daryl got blamed for when they were growing up. He told me I couldn't believe what Daryl said, and that Daryl said things he wanted to believe himself, or wanted others to believe. I kept thinking about that when Daryl opened up to me today. I wondered if I should believe him, especially when he pointed the finger at Ben."

Lucinda agreed. "That's what it all comes down to, doesn't it?"

"Not easy," I said.

"But, if Daryl will sign a statement, we at least have them both for stealing Betsy's body. We need to get Daryl to come in and tell his story to me and make it official. I assume he can take us to wherever they buried Betsy's body," she said.

"But, as for Sheri's case, we have nothing other than Daryl's belief Ben must have done it and Mike must have been involved in the clean-up," I said.

Lucinda shook her head slowly. "I always knew Daryl had something to do with Betsy's death. I was sure of it. I thought it was more than body-snatching, though. A part of me still does, or wants to."

She studied the tabletop thoughtfully. "I didn't realize all that has been going on with that bunch at the church. Although, I've never had much of anything to do with them, either. I was aware of Pastor Martin's past, but I didn't know he'd effectively brought his old organization with him," she said.

I looked up, suddenly aware that Lucinda had stopped talking, and was staring at me across the patio table.

"What?" I asked.

"So, who do you believe? Daryl, or his half-brother, Ben?" she said.

I was slow giving her my answer, which said something in itself. "I've had some questions about all that," I said. "And, in some ways, it's easier to believe Ben, because he's pretty slick compared to Daryl. On the other hand, knowing Ben's a used car salesman, and knowing Daryl better than I do Ben, I'd have to go with believing what Daryl has told me. He really had his heart in what he said. All the stuff Ben told me helps me understand why Daryl is kind of an oddball. But, the more I've gotten to know him, the more I believe him."

"She nodded her head slowly, while looking at me with a mixture of acceptance of what I had said, and something else.

"Well, we've got Daryl and his half-brother for stealing Betsy's body and interfering with her murder investigation. I'll talk to the D.A. and have them both brought in.

This was what I had been dreading. I didn't want Daryl hauled into jail, now that he had finally developed enough trust to tell me what he knew. I thought about the look on his face when Daryl told me how his older half-brother had always convinced people he had done things he claimed Ben himself had done.

"Given Daryl's version of how things went when they were kids, Ben will give Daryl up for anything and everything, whether it's true or not," I said. "And his credibility is going to be hard to challenge. He's a solid member of the church, and Daryl has a questionable juvenile history. I don't see how Daryl can get a fair break with this."

"Life's like that, sometimes," she said. "People sometimes get away with things."

Her face turned grim and determined. "Did Daryl say anything that implicates Chief MacDonald in any of this?" she said. "Anything at all?"

I shook my head. "I didn't ask him directly, but no, he didn't say anything that puts the chief into the picture. I know Pastor Martin said the Chief attends meetings sometimes, but Daryl didn't mention him at all, in any way."

We sat for several minutes, taking a sip or two of wine without talking, or even looking at each other.

"I'm having serious second thoughts about having ever let you get involved in this," Lucinda said. "It has gotten a lot more dangerous. I hope you realize that."

"I do," I said. "But I can't walk away now."

She said she would prefer to pull me out of the investigation entirely, but she was going to let me have one final shot at working with Daryl. Instead of having the police bring him and Ben in for questioning, she was going to let me try to coax Daryl into coming into the station to tell his story to her. She said she couldn't give me much time, though, and she made it clear she didn't want me going back to the church to connect with him. I told her I might be able to catch Daryl at home, or the diner, and said I'd give it a try.

Suddenly, I heard a bell ding, and realized a timer had gone off in the kitchen. Miguella called out that desert was ready, and Lucinda stood up and put her hand on my forearm.

"Just watch yourself," she said.

CHAPTER FORTY

LUCINDA HAD CAUTIONED me against saying too much about my conversation with Daryl to anybody else. Nevertheless, I thought Jeanine and Anne both sensed things were coming to a head, and that I was not altogether upbeat about what I had learned in my meeting with Daryl. I told them my conversation had raised questions, as well as answering some.

"I'm having trouble knowing what to think, at the moment," I said.

We sat around the campfire and tried talking about their day. I described the route to Jerome and talked about the restoration of the old town. In truth, I couldn't get my mind very far off my thoughts about Daryl, the two murdered girls, and the next course of action for me.

Jeanine, and I continued watching the fire turn to coals while Anne volunteered to make coffee. When it was finished, we all sipped our coffee without bothering to attempt much in the way of further conversation. I contributed a nightcap of bourbon. Jeanine and Anne couldn't keep from yawning, and I urged them to turn in.

"I'll probably sit up a while," I said. "I've still got some thinking I need to do."

They accepted my suggestion without protest, and I spent the next hour or so grappling with my thoughts while the embers slowly dissolved into ash.

Next morning, I was up early. I made coffee and shared a quick cup with Jeanine—Anne wasn't up yet—and, then I went into town, hoping to catch Daryl. He wasn't at his apartment, so I tried the diner. When I pulled open the glass door, a wave of warm, syrupy smells announced home-on-the-highway. No sign of Daryl, though. I was glad to see at least one familiar face at the long counter. Rudy, the mountain man, was sitting in the area I usually sat at, and there were a couple of empty stools beside him. I sat down on the one next to him and said hello.

"Ah, my young pilgrim. And, how goes your quest?" he said.

"That's a good question," I said. "Sometimes I'm reminded of that old saying, 'be careful of what you ask for'."

He gave me a quizzical smile and waited.

"I started off just trying to get some information, find out if what I had heard was the truth in any way."

"I remember," he said.

"Well, sometimes you get information you weren't expecting. Now, I have to sort it all out and decide what to believe. Again."

He chuckled. His plump features danced in a display of good humor, and I found myself feeling relieved to be talking with him.

"In this case, it's not like I've found the missing piece to a puzzle," I said. "It's not a game at all. Not that I ever thought it was."

Rudy took hold of his coffee mug, but didn't raise it to his lips. Instead, he sat patiently and let me talk.

"There are some serious issues at stake," I said. "People's lives. I need to stay in the picture, but it's critical I get it right, otherwise someone is going to end up getting hurt."

"That all makes perfect sense," he said. "But, you seem to have come to some critical juncture in your journey, and have encountered the inevitable choice of action you must take."

"I guess you could put it that way," I said. "And, whatever I end up doing will likely be for keeps."

He nodded and sipped his coffee. Carrie, the waitress I met the first time I came to the restaurant, interrupted by bringing me a mug of coffee and taking my breakfast order. I waited until she left before continuing.

"As I was saying, it's all for keeps, and I'm very concerned about getting anyone hurt from my nosing around."

"I take it, that includes your having an awareness of the risks to your own well-being," he said.

"Right now, I'm more concerned about a few others."

"As well you should be," he said. "Although, just to be sure you understand... no quest promises well-being—for anyone involved. Answers. Discovery. Truth. These are the goals of a quest, and ultimately all one can truly hope to gain. The rest is uncertain, and not yours to determine, or yours to control."

He studied me for a moment without saying anything. I had the very unsettling feeling that he was weighing whether or not he wanted to let me in on another of his intuitions, or whatever you'd call them.

"But tell me," he said, after a while. "Who is the focus of these concerns you feel?"

"Another young girl at that church," I said. "Same age as the one who was murdered. In fact, they were friends."

"I see," he said.

"I'm concerned about her, and anyone else who spends too much time around me. And, I'm concerned about Daryl," I said. "He got me started on all this, and I don't want him to pay too big a price for having done it."

Chapter Forty-one

IT WAS BIBLE Study night. Daryl hadn't shown up at the diner for breakfast, or at his apartment later in the day when I checked back again. I hoped he might make it to the Bible study meeting. He had last week. Of course, Lucinda had made it clear I should stay away from the church, and I had no doubts that Pastor Martin, for other reasons, would prefer the same. Trouble was, I had a strong feeling that something was about to happen, and time was fast running out. I had to weigh my options and do the best I could. To me, there really didn't seem to be anything other than going to the Bible study meeting. I needed to contact Daryl with Lucinda's request.

I made sure I was early again. This was going to be tricky, but it was the best way I could think of to connect with Daryl right away. Deacon Thomas was at the church when I got there, and looked surprised but pleased to see I was still coming around. He said he'd loan me a Bible for the night, a version he thought I might like to get for myself, if I continued to seek the Word.

"When you buy your own, you'll want to be able to be able to take notes and write in the margins, as well as highlight passages," he said. "But, please don't mark up the one I'm loaning you. It's only temporary."

I assured him I wouldn't. After all, what would I write down? The names of the people I now considered likely murderers?

I gave Deacon Thomas a hand setting up the chairs again. When they were arranged in a long circle, I told him I was going to get something off my bike and went outside. The girls in the choir were arriving, and Teresa came along on foot, as usual. She waved at me.

"How's it going," I asked.

She smiled and said she was okay, but her eyes didn't light up as she said it.

"That was hard, Sunday," she said. "Singing hymns for Sheri's service without just standing there and crying my eyes out was almost more that I could manage."

Her voice cracked a little, and I sensed that she was still holding a lot of her grief inside—maybe more than just grief.

She pulled a handkerchief out of her jeans pocket and carefully dabbed around her eyes, then blew her nose. When she spoke, her voice barely made it out of her mouth. "I should have been with her," she said. "I never should have left her here alone."

"You probably couldn't have prevented what happened," I said. "And, you might have been hurt yourself."

She shook her head forcefully, as though I was getting all wrong what she wanted to say. "I knew she would get herself into trouble."

"You needed to think about your own safety," I said.

She shrugged. "I hate coming here anymore."

"Why not just drop out of the choir, then? Tell your dad what's going on, and stop coming to church here at all."

"My father would explode," she said. "He wouldn't let me quit. If I stop coming to church, he'll think I'm getting into trouble doing something else."

She shook her head and chuckled softly. "Isn't that a laugh? He believes the only way I'll keep safe is if I keep coming to church. For him, 'safe' means staying a virgin. And, virgins go to church."

For a minute, I thought she might say more, but instead, she said she had to join the other choir members and hurried off toward the open doorway. I glanced around to see if anyone had been watching us. I didn't think anyone had, and felt relieved. Thank God for that much.

CHAPTER FORTY-TWO

IN THE CHURCH meeting room, I took a chair that would let me see the study group members as they came down the hallway. Those who noticed me looked friendly enough, although something in the air was very different. Gary gave me a smile that seemed a little wooden, distracted. He said it was good to see me back again, but his voice carried no enthusiasm. Mike paused in his visual sweep of the room, but he registered no show of surprise, or any other emotion. I guessed that ability came from his prison experience. I wondered if he even had emotions anymore. Others seemed aware of my being there, but avoided eye contact.

Pastor Martin came in among the last of the arrivals again, and looked at me as if to say he was amused to see me back in the game. I kept an eye out for Daryl, but he hadn't shown up by the time Deacon Thomas called the group to order. Pastor Martin led in an opening prayer. He sounded hesitant in his delivery, and somehow communicated a guardedness that spread out and settled over the group like a blanket of caution.

As before, the group was invited to share whatever they might have on their mind and wanted scriptural help with. The same guy who kicked off the last meeting chuckled and spoke up as though he assumed it was his role to go first.

"My wife did better on the headaches, this week—I bought a bottle of the kind of wine she likes best, and she may have gotten just a little drunk. I think that helped."

The rest all laughed, and I could almost feel some of the tension flowing out of the circle. I was kind of surprised they accepted drinking as an okay thing for their members.

Ben grinned at the speaker and quoted some scripture, "'Go thy way, eat thy bread with joy, and drink thy wine with a merry heart'... Ecclesiastes."

That got a good laugh. Then Deacon Thomas mentioned I was back, continuing my journey toward the Lord. Nobody laughed, or commented in any way. I felt my guard go up.

Pastor Martin suggested the group might like to hear what I had learned from my first visit. I thought about possible answers as quickly as I could. I shrugged and tried to grin as I looked around the circle.

"My biggest impression was that it will take a lot of study before I can hope to know the Bible like you all do," I said.

A few smiled and nodded their heads.

Pastor Martin didn't let it stop there. "I believe Mr. Navarro has had more than one purpose in coming to our meetings... more than just learning what the Lord has to say."

I felt the blood draining from my face. It was clear, I wasn't going to get away with enjoying a seamless reentry into the group tonight.

"I'm afraid he is more interested in spreading false statements about us, than in studying the Word," Pastor Martin said.

Deacon Thomas lowered his gaze and looked uncomfortable. Daryl's half-brother, Ben, turned toward me, his expression sober, his stare penetrating. He led off with another Bible quote, this one directed at me. "'So put away all malice and all deceit and hypocrisy... and all slander,'" he said.

I sat, wondering what was coming next. I sneaked a glimpse around the circle. About half had their heads down, like kids in a classroom when the teacher gets on one student's case and the rest don't want to be noticed and become next. Pastor Martin let the awkward tension in the air build for a minute or two.

"'Whoever meddles in a quarrel not his own is like one who takes a passing dog by the ears.' That's from Proverbs," Pastor Martin said. "I think we all know what a passing dog might do to someone who tried to grab it by the ears."

A ripple of meaningful laughter passed through the circle like an electric current.

"That Pit Bull of mine would likely chew his nuts off," one of the men said.

The earlier chuckling was replaced by loud, heartfelt laughter. I cringed at the image the Pit Bull produced in my own mind.

Deacon Thomas straightened in his seat, looked around the circle and added his contribution. "'Whoever goes about slandering reveals secrets, but he who is trustworthy in spirit keeps a thing covered.' Also from Proverbs," he said.

Well, that's it then. They're saying they have a spy in the group—me—so people need to watch what

*they say, and don't give me anything I might be af-
ter.*

I heard several amens mumbled from different lo-
cations. Then Martin said, "Well, I think we're all
clear on where things stand at the moment. I'm sure
others have issues they'd like to give some attention
to."

A shuffling of bibles and boots rippled through the
group as if in response to Martin's indication that the
subject of my presence had been adequately covered.
The rest of the meeting continued about as I remembered from the first time around, with due caution,
however, so as not to give anything away that their
'spy' might pick up on.

When it was over, I stood up and folded my chair,
then carried it into the robing room. Gary followed
with a couple more chairs. He drew close, nearly
brushing against me as he headed toward the stack of
folded chairs, and spoke like he must have been talking out of the side of his mouth.

"I tried to give you the word, man. You could have
fit in and been accepted by everybody. You had your
chance to do things right," he said.

I looked at him, but checked my impulse to say
Sheri Norton and Betsy Horvath hadn't been given
much of a chance, as far as I could tell. He placed his
chairs on the stack and walked off as though nothing
at all had taken place between us. I stacked my chair
on top of the others and stepped into the hallway,
thinking I'd best take off and let things settle out
however they were going to with the study group.
Pastor Martin intercepted me instead. He said he'd
like to have a word with me. He paused to let most of
the rest wrap up and clear out, then nodded toward

the exit. I went along, following a little to the side and a couple of steps in back. I was aware of Mike and Gary bringing up the rear, behind me. When we cleared the doorway and stepped into the parking lot, Pastor Martin stopped and turned to face me. The other two stayed between me and the door we had just come out of.

"We've had our share of troublemakers," Pastor Martin said. "Know how to handle them, too. We've had experience. You might want to keep that in mind."

"Trouble makers? I think I've been behaving pretty well," I said.

"Look, why don't you just get on your bike and hit the road," Pastor Martin said. "You came sniffing around here, looking for Daryl King, or anyone who might tell you whatever it is you're after, and you insist on coming back. These people are my flock. I look after them. Mike and Gary help with that. We have no intention of letting you poke around and cause trouble. These people have enough to deal with without some outsider's meddling. I thought Police Chief MacDonald made that clear to you the other day."

I didn't say anything. The silence hung suspended in the air. Pastor Martin stiffened and squared his shoulders. He heaved a big sigh and spoke again, his voice quiet and tired-sounding.

"Look, I used to ride and raise hell, myself. I rode with a bunch that would chew you up and piss you out just for the fun of it. Two of them are right behind you. I'll pound your ass into the ground myself, if I have to, and not break a sweat doing it. But, I'm trying everything I can to avoid that shit, just to put the matter plain enough, hoping you might get the message."

When he finished, he shrank back to his normal size, which was plenty big enough. He was bigger than me anyway, and a good forty pounds heavier.

A hardened grin creased his face. "I was into anything and everything that would get me into trouble. And, it did. But, I served my nickel and it gave me time to give things some serious thought."

"Five years should provide enough time for that," I said.

Pastor Martin continued. "I found Grace right there inside a barbed wire womb. I was reborn. I found the Lord."

He took a breath, and let it out in a satisfied sigh. He reminded me of Rudy when he talked about the mountains, except Rudy was more convincing.

"I found the Lord, and discovered my calling, the reason I was put on this earth. Now I'm here to serve the flock the Lord has sent me to look after. I will do whatever it takes to accomplish this calling," Pastor Martin said.

"You and your goon squad," I said.

Pastor Martin snorted. "Two good men who also have found their way, and now wish to serve the Lord."

I felt the contents of my gut stir in disgust at Pastor Martin's insistence that he, Mike and Gary were doing anything but serving themselves. Their "flock" seemed to me like a bunch of sheep being herded around by a pack of wolves.

"With two of that flock raped and murdered, you're not doing a very good job of looking after them," I said.

His face darkened. "You're through here, Navarro. Don't come back to any more meetings, and don't come back to this church."

The muscles in the back of my neck tensed. I felt pressure from the swollen area on the back of my head where the bartender hit me with the sap. A little voice in my subconscious chided me for having come here at all tonight, against Lucinda's orders. Then, a faint shuffle of footsteps behind me signaled that Mike or Gary was on the move. I turned halfway around to capture the two within my peripheral vision.

"Not tonight," Pastor Martin said, loud enough for Mike and Gary to hear. "Not tonight, and not here."

He stared at me and spoke in a low, determined voice. "Like I said, Navarro, get on your bike and leave. Leave this church. Leave this town. This is the only warning you're getting."

Pastor Martin stepped to the side, giving me room to pass.

As I reached my bike, I heard a door slam. I looked back, and saw Pastor Martin and his bodyguards were no longer standing there. I glanced around in a reflexive scan of the parking lot, just to make sure no one else was there, and that Teresa wasn't hiding in the shadows, waiting until it was clear to walk home. Then I remembered, I had heard the choir members leaving earlier, before the study group broke up. I hoped she had made it home okay.

CHAPTER FORTY-THREE

I WAS AFRAID I had bungled my whole effort to help Lucinda with her investigation. Instead of helping, I felt I had merely put others in greater danger. I had to make things right, but had no clue as to how. I left the church and cut across town to the access road to pick up the Highway 40 onramp heading east. When problems pile up, I get white line fever, not to run away, but to figure things out. After a few miles, or sometimes hours, I usually start thinking better.

As the onramp merged with the highway, I glanced to the side to see if anything was coming that I didn't think I could outrun and twisted the throttle open. My bike has a lot of low end torque, and winding up through the gears took me on the highway at a speed that would put almost anything coming along out of contention. I checked in the rearview, just in case. Nothing. I had the road to myself. The night wind was chill and smelled fresh with a scent of pine. My straight pipes made the perfect accompaniment to my mood, and the black asphalt called me forward. I settled back on the seat and hoped the open-road medicine would do its work this time. But, how do you get over feeling like a traitor?

I knew it had been my idea to join the stupid Bible Study group so I could find out more about what was going on at the church. That had caused more harm than good. After all, my so-called cover was blown, or had never been established that well in the first place. I was pretty sure most of the group members were just a bunch of good old boys using the meetings as a sort of night out, but some were using it for much worse. Trouble is, they were dipping below the eligibility line when they hit on the underage choirgirls, and going beyond the point of no-return when they fell to rape and covered it with murder.

I drove on for another few miles before I began to see, rather than sense, the night images coming into view in the flood of light from my headlamps. I'm always alert to things along the side of the highway like a deer ready to run across. But, you can be alert to background without actually *seeing* what's there. The lighted trunks of pine trees began standing out as spires against darkened forest. They rose tall, mystical pillars guarding a magical kingdom. A few visible stars overhead confirmed the night ceiling still vaulted into infinity, more grand than any church I'd ever been in.

After a few minutes, I began feeling the chill from the wind whipping against my skin. The hypnotic white line segments plastered along the center of the highway lured me on into the night, but I realized it was time I turned back. I could breathe again. I hadn't erased all the bad feelings I'd started off with, but I hadn't expected that much to happen. With a deep sigh of resignation, I slowed down until I could pull a U-turn and headed back to the campground. I had done nearly all I could do on my quest, as Rudy called it, but not everything. I still had Lucinda's request to bring Daryl in.

When I got to the campground, Jeanine and Ann had a campfire going and were sitting near it, drinking a glass of wine. They invited me to join them.

"Bring your cup," Ann said.

I dug out my porcelain mug and accepted their offer.

"How was your meeting?" Jeanine asked. She was sitting propped on her forearms, which rested on her knees.

I gave them the story.

"So, you've done everything you can do. Now the police will finish the job. You don't have to go back there and expose yourself to that dangerous bunch anymore."

I picked up a stick and poked at some burning embers, piling them into the center of the fire. I could hear the concern in Jeanine's voice, and knew her advice was sound, even though I knew I couldn't follow it.

"There are still some things for me to," I said. "Once I figure out the best way to handle them. I feel worried about Daryl. He trusted me enough to open up and talk. When he did, I still had doubts about whether I should believe him or his step brother. To make things worse, now he's put himself in real danger by talking with me. I don't think anyone knows how much he's told me, but that may not help enough."

"Bobby, you tried to convince me a while back that this is not the Wild West," Jeanine said. "Perhaps you need to tell yourself that as well. You cannot walk down the main street of town in front of the saloon and face all the bad guys by yourself. This is why you have a police force. You're a civilized nation now."

I laughed at her description of me, and felt a little embarrassed that she might be right. Well, partially right, anyway. Then I thought about Pastor Martin, and his outfit using a church for their own benefit, and running it like an outlaw gang.

"It's not the Wild West, but there are still issues with what some people do—and get away with," I said. "And, I feel responsible for any mess I've made that makes it worse."

"Oh, you're impossible!" she said. "I can't talk to you, if you're not going to listen to reason."

With that, Jeanine got up and stalked off to their tent. I watched her climb inside, then stared at the fire again, asking myself what all had just happened.

CHAPTER FORTY-FOUR

NEXT MORNING, JEANINE was speaking to me at least, but she was still pissed at my stubbornness. I had made coffee, and she accepted a cup. I told her I was going to grab breakfast at the diner, in the hope of catching up with Daryl.

"I don't know what we're going to do today yet," she said. "I'll have to talk with Anne, when she gets up."

I finished my coffee, and drove into town. This time, I was lucky. Daryl was at the counter in his usual place. He glanced at me as I sat down on the stool next to him, but kept eating.

"Ready to order, hon?" Carrie, the waitress, said.

I told her what I wanted, and she left to put the order in and bring some coffee.

"I went to the Bible study thing last night," I said to Daryl. "I didn't see you around."

He turned to look at me without answering.

"I guess word is out that I'm a spy in camp," I said. "They made a bunch of scripture comments to make it official to everyone. I guess you could say I'm now persona non grata. After the meeting, Pastor Martin let me know I wasn't welcome to come back anymore. Actually, he suggested I get the hell out of Dodge."

Daryl's expression became thoughtful. "What all did they say?" he asked.

"Pastor Martin let me know he'd done some time, and had experience dealing with people who rock the boat. Told me he didn't like my snooping around, and said it was none of my business."

"Say anything about me?" Daryl asked.

This was the part I dreaded. "He made it clear he knew I'd started hanging around hoping I could talk with you, or anyone else I could get to open up."

"What did you tell him?"

"Not much. He wasn't there to listen, just give me a message. He told me to stay away."

Daryl slurped his coffee and finished chewing on the mouthful he had been working on before we started talking. Carrie set my coffee down, and I gratefully took a sip. It tasted good, and was what I needed, but too hot to drink yet. I set the mug down and looked at Daryl.

"I didn't say anything to back up their suspicions. Didn't need to. I don't know what they think I've found out, but I have to say I think you should watch out for your own ass. From what you told me, they don't play around. And... I believe what you told me."

Daryl stared deep into my eyes for a minute. "You mean that?" he said.

I nodded. "I believe you. I believe everything you told me."

He took another slurp of coffee and sighed, as though a weight had been partially lifted.

"But, I think you need to protect yourself," I said. "I also think the best way to do that is to finish the job."

"What do you mean?"

"I want you to tell the police everything you told me. It's the only way they can do anything about it.

And, deep down, that's what you want... for them to do what has to be done to stop this from happening again. And to make up for what has already happened."

Daryl stared at his plate, his expression grim but determined.

"I knew one of the officers in high school," I said. "She's interested in finding out what really happened. All of it. I've told her what I could, but she needs to hear it from you."

"You told her the stuff I said to you?"

I nodded. "I had to," I said. "It's the only way this is going to get straightened out."

For a minute, I didn't know if he was going to stomp off, or clam up and go Daryl on me. Something of the old panic registered in his eyes and his mouth quivered, like he was about to start mumbling to himself. I hoped he didn't. I didn't want to lose him after everything it had taken to get this far. Carrie poured him some more coffee, studying his face, but not saying anything. I kind of held my hand up, as much to signal her to go away as to say I didn't need any more coffee at the moment. She retreated to the serving counter.

"You need to do it for Betsy," I said.

CHAPTER FORTY-FIVE

OUTSIDE, HEAT RADIATED up from the sidewalk, baking my jeans against my thighs, and I could feel the skin on my arms grow damp with sweat. I had called Lucinda's number, and left a message for her to get back to me. The plan with Daryl was that I would I would set up the meeting with Lucinda. Then, I'd meet him and we would talk with her together. He still didn't trust the police very much. Now, I just had to wait for her return call.

I turned my attention down the street where I had stopped at Ernesto's car and found Sheri Norton's body. Now, that moment seemed to belong to another lifetime, but, at least now things were finally coming together. Once Daryl made his statement official, the police would be able to find Betsy Horvath's body, bring Ben in, and likely Mike as well. There was still work to be done, but as far as the two murder investigations were concerned, Betsy's and Sheri's, things were beginning to look promising.

Of course, I still felt nervous about everything rolling out as hoped. Daryl might revert to his old ways and change his mind about talking, but I didn't think that would likely happen. It had taken a lot of courage for him to go this far, and he seemed determined to see it through—for Betsy's sake. I pulled my phone out and checked to make sure the ringer was set on max and the battery was okay. It wasn't charged fully, but probably had enough juice in it. I jammed the phone back in my pocked. I've never been good at waiting.

On impulse, I walked down to the store where the old geezer had stood in the doorway thinking I was the one responsible for the stench of a dead body outside. I went in and looked around. There were some tea shirts hanging on one of the walls behind a counter. I started reading the designs on them, but got distracted by a shuffling motion toward the back of the store. It was the old geezer himself, carefully making his way down the aisle toward me.

I pointed toward a shirt with a Native American design on it. "Nice shirt," I said.

He nodded. "Twenty dollars," he said.

I thought about it. You have to be careful how much you buy when you ride a bike and have a long way to go.

The old man frowned. "You look familiar."

I gave him my best friendly smile. "You might remember me from a while back, when that girl was murdered and her body was found in a car right outside."

I smiled again and turned my head toward him. "You thought I was the one who had left the car there."

He continued to stare at me, slowly shaking his head from side to side.

"That's what you told the police," I said.

He continued shaking his head. "I never said nothing like that to no police. They asked if I saw anything, and I told them I didn't see nothing."

"You didn't tell the police I parked the car and tried to leave it?"

He shook his head some more.

"I didn't say nothing like that. Why would I? I never saw when it was put there."

I paid the old man for the shirt, wondering who did tell the cops I was the one who left Ernesto's car there. Did Detective Alvarez just make that story up to rattle my cage and get me talking? Well, no matter now. I had other things on my mind, like Lucinda returning my call. In that regard, my phone had started ringing. I pulled it out of my pocket and saw the caller was Lucinda.

"Good news," I said, when I got outside to the sidewalk. "Daryl's willing to give you his statement in person."

"Hello to you too," she said.

I laughed and went on to tell her Daryl said he wanted me to come with him, and that he was to meet me at the diner in the morning and we would go wherever she wanted from there. She said that would be fine, and to meet her at the police station. We agreed on a time.

"Well, that's good. Maybe we can crack this thing," she said. "I'm sure it wasn't easy for Daryl to agree to this, any more than it was easy for him to tell you about it in the first place. "I hope he realizes, he's implicating himself in connection with some serious charges. It's not just pointing a finger at his half-brother."

"He understands that," I said. "He just wants to put things right. What happened to Sheri was a tipping point. It was what happened to Betsy Horvath, all over again."

"Well, you've done a terrific job, Bobby. Just bring him in to make his statement in the morning, and hopefully we'll be able to push this through to a conclusion."

CHAPTER FORTY-SIX

WITH THINGS SET up for Daryl and me to meet Lucinda, I felt a sense of relief and nervous apprehension at the same time. I just hoped nothing would go wrong. I wanted to get it over with. And, I didn't know what to do with myself in the meantime.

I put the Tee shirt I had bought from the old geezer into a saddlebag and drove back to the campground. I could see the girls hadn't left yet. Their rental car was still there, and Jeanine was poking around, doing something at the picnic table. I parked on my side and dropped the kickstand.

"Good news," I said. "I was able to catch up with Daryl, and he agreed to meet with my friend, Lucinda."

"That is good," Jeanine said. "Now you have no excuse to do anymore Old West stuff."

I laughed. "No more Wild West."

I lifted the coffee pot to see if anything might be left. It felt like I might squeeze a swallow or two out of the remains, so I dug out a mug, after making sure Jeanine didn't intend to finish it off herself.

"What are you to up to today? Anne must be up by now, isn't she?"

Jeanine jerked her head toward the camp store. "She's taking a shower," she said. "We've been arguing over what we should do for ourselves today. I didn't feel like doing much of anything."

"Oh? How come? Just feel like kicking back?"

She shrugged and made a face. "What about you?" she asked.

I told her I hadn't made any plans beyond trying to find Daryl. Now, all I had to do was meet him at the diner again in the morning.

Anne had emerged from the shower room by that time, and was nearing the campsite.

"We were just comparing our plans for the day," I said. "So far, nobody has any."

Anne smirked and said, "She was just worried you were going to get yourself into some kind of trouble again. She didn't want to leave the campground, in case you did."

Jeanine blushed and looked shocked at Anne's accusation. I was totally surprised myself, but I couldn't say altogether displeased, either.

"Hey, how would you two like to visit an Indian ruin?" I said. "Montezuma's Castle isn't too far, and it's easy to get to. It's beautiful. If you like, we could all go together."

They both thought the idea sounded great. We agreed we had to take their car, as the bike would only carry two at the most.

Montezuma's Castle National Monument is near Sedona, a beautiful area of red sandstone cliffs and expensive real estate. The "castle" is an impressive five-story high set of cliff dwellings built into some cavernous openings in the sheer face of a cliff by ancient Sinagua natives. The walls of the dwellings are plastered over, giving the whole an appearance of being whitewashed. While visitors cannot go inside the ruins, you can get a good view of them from a foot-path leading through a grove of sycamore trees. You know you're at a tourist site, a very popular one, but you can still stand at the edge of the path and become drawn into the ancient dwellings and feel a sense of awe at what was done there.

Jeanine and Anne both seemed to enjoy the cliff dwellings. While they looked through the visitor center gift shop, it was clear they appreciated the ancient monument more than the souvenirs, by far. After-ward, we had lunch in Sedona, and they indulged in an exploration of the ton of shops open and compet-ing to snare a few tourist dollars. I tagged along and tried to appear to be enjoying myself too. I'm not a big shopper.

If you know how to find the route, you can take a road from Sedona that takes you through Oak Creek Canyon, a beautiful, twisting climb up, to Flagstaff. We ended up having dinner at a Mexican restaurant in Flagstaff, and getting back to the campground late, tired, but thoroughly satisfied with the day. As Anne pulled to a stop at the edge of their campsite, the campground manager came rushing out of the camp store, waving her arms and hollering at us.

"Where have you folks been all day?" she said.

We climbed out of the car, confused as to what her problem might be.

"Your motorcycle was here all day, but we had no idea where you were." Her comment was directed at me, and she seemed put out that I hadn't left word where I was going, or how to reach me.

"The police have been trying get hold of you," she said.

CHAPTER FORTY-SEVEN

"A PHONE CALL came in to the office," the hostess said. "They said they were the police, and they needed to get hold of you. They said they tried phoning your cell phone, and it wasn't working."

The battery hadn't lasted as long as I thought it would.

"They gave me a phone number, and told me to let you know you should call it as soon as I saw you."

She thrust her hand into a pocket on the front of her apron and brought out a slip of paper. "Here," she said. "You have to call this number."

I checked my phone to verify that it was dead, and told the manager I'd have to use a phone in the office. I followed her inside and dialed the number she had given me. It seemed familiar, but I couldn't say who it belonged to. I thanked the manager and waited while the phone rang at the other end. The manager hovered close by. I wished I could use my cellphone; I'd be able to go outside and enjoy a little privacy. The ringing stopped, and a voice came on at the other end.

"Bobby, I'm glad they were able to reach you."

The voice belonged to Lucinda.

"I'm afraid I have some bad news," she said. "A body was found today, just off the access highway out of town. The ME is still working at his end, and we don't have an official identification yet, but I saw who it was. It looks like Daryl King was beaten to death and his body dumped out by the highway."

I was stunned by Lucinda's announcement, and sickened by what I was sure happened. I didn't see the body myself; I didn't have to. Lucinda's brief description told me about all I needed to know. She said the ME had taken the body for examination, and the scene had been investigated. Evidently the beating had taken place somewhere else. She couldn't say what time, exactly. She suggested I meet her at her office.

"Things are busy as hell around here, and kind of topsy-turvy," she said. "I won't be able to meet with you long, but we can talk for a few minutes."

Outside, I told Jeanine I had to take care of another emergency and would fill them in later, then climbed on my bike. In town, I parked my bike on the street, and went inside the outer foyer of the police station. The officer on duty buzzed me inside and led me to Lucinda's desk. She had already poured two coffees, and had them waiting.

"Whoever did it was pretty methodical," she said, when I sat down. "I didn't see evidence on Daryl's body to suggest he had put up much of a defense."

"Did it look like he'd been tied up, or just beaten to death?"

She shook her head. "No ligature marks. Looks like person, or persons, worked him over a bit, then broke his neck. I think they knew what they were doing, and how to get it done."

I cradled the Styrofoam cup in my hands. It was too hot to drink. Lucinda reached across the desk and put her hand on my wrist.

"I don't think it went on and on," she said. "It was still a terrible thing to happen, but it didn't look as though he had to suffer as long as these things sometimes last."

"That's something," I said. It was, but it wasn't much.

"He may even have been unconscious when his neck was broken."

"Any evidence you can use?"

"It's too early to say, yet. The Medical Examiner may be able to pull some DNA from the body. Hard to be certain at this point."

I stared off to the side, toward another desk with an officer apparently calling numbers from a rolodex, one by one. The image I had conjured up of Daryl's body, then of Daryl getting beaten to death, kept pushing aside the real image of the officer at the other desk, and I kept fighting the imagined image of Daryl's murder.

"You know as well as I do who did this," I said.

She gave my wrist a little squeeze. "You stay completely out of it, Bobby. You'll only cause trouble, and get into trouble yourself."

Her voice was firm, businesslike. I sat there, saying nothing, feeling numb, but with a sickening rage bubbling deep inside.

"This happened because of me—the things I've been doing to find out what happened to Sheri Norton," I said.

"Don't start doing that. This happened because a murderer targeted Daryl," Lucinda said.

I shook my head. "I got him to trust me. Trust me enough to tell me what happened. That bunch at the

church knew he was talking, and they shut him up…
just like they warned him they would."

"You still can't blame yourself."

"He didn't show up at the diner the other day, so I
did exactly what you warned me not to do. I went to
the Bible Study meeting."

Lucinda's expression froze. She stared at me without saying anything.

"They made it clear, with a bunch of Bible quotes,
that they knew I'd been hanging around to spy on
them. Afterward, Pastor Martin and his two goons escorted me outside and told me not to come back. Pastor Martin said they knew I had been looking for
Daryl, and snooping around to talk with anybody I
could get to open up. He said it was the only warning
I'd get."

We both sat not talking for several minutes. Then,
her phone chimed, and she fished it out of her pocket
and listened. The message, discussion, or whatever,
was short, and when it was done she put her phone
back and quietly said, "Gotta go. I'll talk to you later.
As soon as I can."

I got up and followed her out to the entryway,
where she left me on my own. My bike still sat at the
curb, but it seemed almost foreign as I climbed into
the saddle. Was this a reaction to my having gotten
Daryl killed? Or was I just punishing myself for something that would have happened whether I made that
last Bible study meeting or not, as Lucinda insisted
just before we parted?

CHAPTER FORTY-EIGHT

JEANINE AND ANNE came over to my campsite as I pulled up. I also noticed the campground manager had stepped out of the office and appeared to be considering joining us as well. She took a couple of steps our way, then stopped and retreated, but turned at the doorway and stood looking in our direction.

Jeanine said she had put a pot of water on to boil, and that it should be ready for making tea in a couple of minutes. The hissing of the propane made a nice domestic sound, as did the laughter and shouts of some children playing at the far end of the campground. But, to me, sounds of normalcy seemed out of place.

"A cup of tea sounds real good," I said.

Anne fished several teabags out of a container and rounded up some mugs, putting a teabag in each one. Jeanine and I sat at the picnic table. I glanced, and saw the manager still looking at us. Anne poured hot water over the teabags and set them on the table, then sat down.

"Well," I said. "You know the murder case I've been helping out with."

They both nodded attentively.

"And, I told you I had talked with Daryl, and he gave me some breakthrough information. I was supposed to meet him in the morning, so he could make an official statement to the police."

They nodded again in unison.

"Somebody killed him."

They both said, "Oh no!" in one voice, their faces registering horror at my announcement.

"This is awful," Jeanine said. "How did it happen? Tell me he was in an accident. Did someone do this thing on purpose?" Anne asked.

I thought about how to answer her question for a few seconds. I couldn't think of a good way to phrase it. "They beat him to death and broke his neck," I said.

Both Anne and Jeanine shuddered and looked horrified by my statement. Jeanine appeared to trying not to be sick. Anne was the first to recover enough to say anything. "Are you saying this had to do with the other murders you have been involved with?"

"I have to think so," I said.

They looked at each other, their concern evident. "I think this has become a dangerous place for us to be," Anne said, her firm voice a grim announcement. "I think, perhaps it's a dangerous place for you as well, Bobby."

I couldn't think of a good response to Anne's comment. In the distance, a squeal of laughter broke out again. Children, playing with no awareness of people killing each other. Children being children, the way they should be. The camp manager had started walking our way again, and I knew I was going to have to say something about why the police had been looking for me. I didn't want to say much.

"Everything all right, here?" the manager said as she reached our table.

I looked up at her. "The police needed to get ahold of me about someone I know," I said. "There was an incident in town, someone was hurt seriously, and they needed to talk with me. I'm afraid I can't say much more about it, but that's why they were looking for me."

The manager gave me a hard stare for a few seconds. Clearly, she wanted more information. She planted her feet wide and crossed her arms over her chest. "That doesn't explain much," she said.

"I'm afraid I don't have a whole lot of information, at this point," I said. "They just needed to talk with me."

I realized I wasn't telling her why the police wanted to talk with me, I couldn't. Jeanine and Anne had picked up on my lead and sat without saying anything. I felt grateful to them.

"We can't run a campground where this sort of thing goes on," the manager said. "I'm going to have to talk with the Mister about this. The police trying to get hold of you, something going on, someone getting seriously hurt. This isn't the sort of thing families want going on at any campground they intend staying at. I can tell you that much."

She uncrossed her arms and moved her hands to the top of her hips. "I'm definitely going to have to talk with the Mister about this," she said.

When I didn't reply, she gave me a last accusing look and returned to the office.

"I wonder how long before they kick me out?" I said.

Anne stood up and unwrapped herself from the bench seat of the picnic table. "I think we should all leave," she said. "There is too much happening here.

Too much dangerous business going on. I think we should all leave and let the police do whatever it is they can do to take care of this."

I felt a huge lump in my throat as Anne's words cut to the chase and brought out the obvious. I had put everyone's life in danger. I had opened a can of horrors, and had no way of putting things right again. I felt sick at the thought of their leaving, even though I had to agree it was the best thing for them to do. Obviously, Mike was doing his clean-up now, and there was no telling how far it would go. Just as clearly, Mike would take it however far he thought it needed to go.

"I hate to say this, but Anne's right," I said.

Jeanine's face was twisted with competing emotions. I felt the same way.

"The last thing I want is for anything to happen to either of you," I said. "This whole thing has gotten out of hand. After what happened to Daryl, I can't say anyone is safe."

"But, what will you do, Bobby?" Jeanine said.

I shook my head. "I haven't got that far," I said. "I'm pretty sure I'm going to get kicked out of here. I can't blame them. I've stirred up a hornet's nest."

Anne looked confused, "Hornet's nest?"

Jeanine said something to her in Norwegian, and Anne nodded in understanding. Then she tossed me a look that seemed to suggest she agreed with the metaphor of what my actions had unleashed. Jeanine reached across the table and took hold of my wrist. "So, you'll go too, Bobby? Leave here before something happens to you?"

"I can't. I'm responsible for this mess. I can't take off and leave it for someone else to clean up."

CHAPTER FORTY-NINE

IN THE MORNING I got up and hit the showers early. I knew I wouldn't be able to get any real sleep once the sun came up and the campground came awake. A couple of other campers were already at the sinks, but there was one open. Naturally, the counter area around the sink was wet, and a gob of toothpaste perched on the edge of the sink where the last person had not bothered to wipe the area down. I took a couple of paper towels from the dispenser and cleaned things up, then opened my shaving kit and got out my toothbrush.

When I finished shaving and showering, I returned to the campsite, feeling cleaner and refreshed, even though no more optimistic about whatever the day might offer. I had spent much of the night thinking about Daryl's death, and the murders of the two girls. I lighted my camp stove and put some coffee on, then started a fire. The sound of a tent zipper announced Jeanine was getting up as well.

"Good morning, Bobby," she said. "Were you able to get any sleep last night?"

I appreciated her sensitivity. I smiled and shrugged. "Some," I said.

She wore a Tee-shirt and pajama bottoms. Her hair was tousled, and hung loose against her neck and shoulders and carried a hint of yesterday's perfume.

"Anne is convinced we must leave," she said.

I nodded. "When will you go?" I asked.

"We have laundry to do, and it will take a while to pack everything. Besides, we haven't even had breakfast yet. But I think we will be ready to leave by lunchtime.

While Jeanine headed for the showers, I began frying bacon and putting together some sourdough biscuits for breakfast. I had already started the eggs by the time Anne crawled out of the sack, stretching and yawning like a Teddy bear. I was going to miss them both, but shared Anne's feeling that things had become too uncertain to feel safe any longer.

The best way to handle a goodbye is with a hug and a smile and a cheerful wave. We exchanged e-mails and phone numbers, and assured each other we would stay in touch. Behind me, I heard a screen door slam, turned and saw Russ walking over toward my campsite as Jeanine and Anne drove off.

"Hey, Russ," I said.

"We have a problem," he said. "People are getting upset and asking what's going on, what with the police after you, and what all."

"That so?" I said.

"We can't have that sort of thing. This is a family campground. We let you come in here for a couple of days because you seemed to need a place to stay. We can't have people getting worried about what all might happen, though. You're going to have to find another place to stay."

I grinned at him and gave some thought to a couple of responses I felt like making, but decided against saying anything."

"If you give me any trouble, I'll just get the Sheriff out here and have you arrested," he said.

"Not necessary, Russ. I'll be out of here in a little while."

He gave me what I supposed was meant to be a stern look of warning, and then returned to the camp store. I looked at the empty campsite where Jeanine and Anne had been a few minutes before. I felt as though a whirlwind had just swept everything that mattered off into the dessert. With a bitter sigh of resignation, I began putting my things together to break camp.

I didn't like the thought of having to spend the extra money, but I needed someplace to stay, and the only place that came to mind was the motel I had been at when I first came to town. They had a vacancy a couple of doors down from my original room, the air conditioner appeared to be working, as well as the TV, so I unloaded my gear, dropped on the bed and stared at the ceiling.

The air conditioner made a loud noise every time the compressor kicked in. Then slowly, a wave of cool air floated over the bed. Some sounds of voices drifted from the end of the wing where my room was located. I remembered seeing a cart stacked with linens and hung with bags of soiled laundry nearby when I checked in. The maid service must still be getting all the rooms ready. I could only catch a few words here and there, but it sounded like two people were busy exchanging gossip as they worked.

I thought about Jeanine and Anne, and wondered how they were making out. As Jeanine had said, their time had become very limited, regardless of Anne's concerns about safety. Still, I had enjoyed their company, especially Jeanine's. I wondered how much we would maintain contact as they got caught up in their new lives at graduate school, and I went back East to what I knew—blasting.

I guess I have to admit, I was working myself into a real funk when my cell phone went off. For a foolish instant, I wondered if it might be Jeanine, just getting in touch.

"Hello?" I said.

"Bobby, I've got some more bad news."

It was Lucinda, and she was calling to tell me I should meet her at the hospital. Teresa Gonzales had been the victim of a hit-and-run accident.

CHAPTER FIFTY

IT DIDN'T TAKE long to get to the hospital. Lucinda was waiting for me in an area off the main entrance and registration desk.

"It happened last night," she said. "I'd heard we had a hit-and-run, but didn't know anything more about it until just a little while ago."

She had stood up to meet me when I came in. Now, she took me by the forearm and suggested we go to the cafeteria and talk over coffee.

"We can't see her now," she said. "The doctors have told me she should be allowed to get some rest. They said if she wakes up they'll let me know, and we might be able to see her for a brief visit."

Feeling numb, I followed Lucinda to the cafeteria. She told the person behind the service counter we'd like two cups of coffee, then looked at me for agreement. I nodded. We carried the coffee to a table in the corner and sat down.

"She must have been coming home from somewhere," Lucinda said. "Maybe some meeting at the church. I was hoping she might wake up before you got here. I'd really like us to be able to talk with her."

"Think she might be able to identify who hit her?"

She shrugged. "That's not very likely, but I'd like to find out where she'd been before it happened, and what she'd been doing."

"Did anybody see it happen? How did you folks get the word?" I said.

"Actually, it was a 911 call. Probably someone in the neighborhood who was afraid to go outside and get involved in person made the phone call."

She took a sip of coffee. Her face looked drawn. I imagined she was exhausted.

"At least they did that much," she said. "They did call 911."

"How could anybody just sit behind the window shades when a young girl is hit and not go out and try to help? Give her first aid?"

"You'd be surprised," she said.

With Daryl's murder, and now Teresa's hit-and-run, it was evident that Mike was cleaning up residue from Sheri Norton's murder—and from my snooping around. Lucinda thought as much, and warned me that I was likely next on his to-do list. She said she had people looking for him, and she hoped to bring him in for questioning, but they hadn't been able to locate him yet. I said I'd keep an eye out and watch my back.

I needed to pick up a couple of things before going back to my motel room, so I drove to a supermarket I had located. At the market, I parked my bike off to the side of the lot, but still near the entrance. I picked up some new razors, toothpaste, and a bag of jerky for snacks. It only took me a few minutes. I put the stuff in a saddlebag on top of some foul weather gear and was just straightening up when my head exploded.

It was like being hit with the sap all over again, except this time I didn't wake up in a clean hospital bed with a friendly face looking over me. I came-to in what I figured out was the covered bed of a pickup truck. It was bouncing down a road, and each bump sent spasms of pain flashing throughout my skull. I could move. I wasn't tied up. But, I couldn't manage to open the tailgate and jump out, either.

I couldn't tell where the truck was, or was headed. It seemed to be moving right along, but I had no idea of how fast. I wasn't used to riding lying down in the bed of a truck. Everything seemed dirty and small plumes of dust stirred up whenever the truck went over a good sized bump in the road. Although my vision had cleared somewhat, there was hardly any light coming into the back of the truck, so I felt, more than saw, that it was littered with loose gear, empty Styrofoam cups, take-home boxes, and empty bottles. I felt around to discover whether anything might serve as a weapon, once the damn thing stopped bouncing around. I found a lug wrench. That and a beer bottle were the best I could find. They would have to do. Then I felt the truck slow down and slew to a stop.

I could hear the driver side door of the cab open and a moment later slam shut again. Nothing opened on the passenger side. The driver cleared his throat and spat. I thought I heard a footstep outside, and guessed he was coming around to the rear of the truck. I pivoted with my legs close to the tailgate. I knew I couldn't just jump out once the backend was opened, due to the fiberglass cover, but maybe I would get lucky and land a kick. I didn't have long to wait before finding out. The locking mechanism on the tailgate turned, then the tailgate swung down, letting in a blinding blast of sunlight. I slammed my feet through the opening, trying to connect with whoever had just dropped the tailgate.

Unfortunately, he was expecting as much, and managed to sidestep my kick, grab my leg and yanked me out onto the ground. I slid partway, then thumped to the ground head-first. The pain from the earlier blow to the back of my head exploded again, but not as bad as when he first hit me back at the parking lot. I tried to roll over and get up. I didn't get very far. He kicked me in the mid-section several times, taking my wind away, sending sheets of pain throughout my groin and stomach. I rolled into a ball as best I could, throwing my arms toward the top of my head to protect my skull. He booted me twice in the kidneys, which I had to leave unprotected.

Neither kick was as solid as it could have been, but it doesn't take much of a blow to the kidneys to get your attention. I tried to tuck my legs closer to my body to protect against a kick to that area, and hoped he'd leave my head alone. To my relief, he stepped back and watched me as I struggled to get my breath and regain some control of my body.

"Should have left town when you had a chance, asshole," he said.

It was Mike, and he had me at a big disadvantage.

"Just hold your shit together for a few minutes," he said. "Gary ought to be here any minute. He's bringing your bike."

"Then what?" I said.

"Then you're going to have an accident. Your bike's going to hit an abutment, and you're going to break a few things… including your neck."

His voice was calm, his statement a simple description of events about to unfold. No excitement.

No nervousness. No threat... just a statement of what was about to happen.

"Don't worry though. You won't feel any of it," Mike said. "You'll already be dead. The crash will make it look like the whole thing happened a little differently than it actually will."

He paused, as though giving me time to say something if I wanted to. The ground beneath me was dry and powdery, a mixture of pine needles and dirt. I rolled onto my back and stretched my legs out a little. My head was halfway under the rear bumper of the pickup, and I could see the dirty leather sack Mike had hung from the trailer hitch with the iron hitch balls in it, giving the effect of a large scrotum. From that vantage point, I could see how the sack was fastened, and that it could be freed by simply pulling the pin for the hitch receiver loose.

Mike continued talking. "I'll take care of the broken neck thing myself," he said. "The rest of it too. Actually, I've kind of been looking forward to this."

"Don't overdo yourself," I said.

"No problem. Just something I'll enjoy taking care of, kind of on a personal basis, so I'll take my time."

For the first time, I heard him chuckle, and a smile altered his expression, even if ever so slightly. Then I heard the rumble of my straight pipes heading in our direction. Gary was coming with my bike, as Mike had said would happen, and the show was about to begin.

CHAPTER FIFTY-ONE

I RAISED MY head and looked toward the sound of the approaching motorcycle with a hypnotic sense of dread. The engine slowed. The bike came into view as it rounded a curve in the road. I had a sudden urge to scramble up and try to knock Gary off the bike as he drove up. Of course, even if I got that far, which was pretty much out of the question with Mike stranding there, the most I could accomplish would result in my bike falling over. It weighs close to a thousand pounds, and you don't just yank something like that upright. As if reinforcing the futility of trying anything like that, Mike kicked me a couple more times, leaving me gasping for breath and paralyzed with pain.

Gary pulled up close to the pickup and stopped, clicked the transmission into neutral, and shut the engine off. The effect of the sudden silence, was to make me acutely aware of my situation, and the need to do anything I could to better my position.

"I don't want to take all day with this," Mike said, turning and taking a couple steps toward Gary.

"I'll take care of big shot here," he said. Then you can help me dump his ass back in the truck and we'll go stage the accident."

"Got it," Gary said.

Realizing this was my only opportunity, I reached up with my right hand and pulled the hitch pin loose as quietly and quickly as I could, grabbing hold of the leather sack with my left. I let the sack and my arms drop to my sides as soon as the pin came free, hoping my movement was not observed.

Gary climbed off the bike and glanced at me without any sign he had noticed my action. Kind of to my surprise, his face registered no emotion at all, not even a sign of recognition. I briefly wondered how he felt about being a part of all this. After all, he had let me know I might be accepted by the group, and later seemed a little disappointed I had made a bad choice by not joining them. Of course, that was then; this was now.

I also had the feeling Gary would do whatever Mike told him to do, and without hesitation, at any time—then, now, or any time in the future. Any feelings Gary still had would be shoved aside whenever Mike gave an order.

Mike turned in my direction; the moment of truth had come. I gathered my legs under me and lunged upright. I feinted toward his head, but dropped down and swung the hitch ball sack at Mike's knees as he stepped toward me. I felt the steel balls make a solid connection with his left knee, and heard the satisfying howl of pain as he dropped.

Gary had already started toward us, probably having thought I'd be likely to make a try at something and anticipating Mike would expect him to move in as backup. Gary thought better of the idea when I hit Mike, who now lay half on the ground with his knee badly damaged. Gary stopped and remained a few feet away. I covered the ground toward him in an instant, while he tried to take in what was happening. He must have expected some kind of action, but I don't think he had figured I would come at them with a weapon.

While Gary tried to take in the new situation, I drew my arm back and brought the hitch ball sack down in a sweeping overhead arc that ended by glancing off the side of his head and onto his collarbone. He went to his knees in a shriek of pain and I whirled to face Mike again.

The fight had turned in my favor, as long as neither of them had a gun, but it wasn't over yet. Not by a long shot. Mike's knee was obviously pretty useless, but he had not stopped fighting. He had managed to stand up again, mostly on his right leg, and to dig a switchblade knife out of his pocket. He lunged at me in a slight crouch, stabbing at my midsection with his knife. I sidestepped.

The hitch ball sack had proven to be a formidable weapon initially, but now it was less effective—harder to use against the knife. Because of the weight of the steel balls, the sack was slow to swing and hard to control compared to a hand or fist, particularly one holding a knife.

Mike's eyes burned with a deep fury as he recovered his balance and faced me, holding his arm cocked at a ninety-degree angle, elbow at his side, the knife blade thrust forward. I stepped to the side, forcing him to have to turn to keep me in front of him in spite of his injured knee.

"I'm still going to kill you," he said. "You just got lucky."

I switched the hitch ball sack to my left hand again, and circled. Mike's face barely registered the pain I suspected his knee must be giving him. I stepped in a little to close the distance between us. Mike made a guttural sound, like an animal growling, and swiped at my midsection. I hunched my belly in, but felt the sharp blade slice through my shirt—and the flesh covering my stomach.

Before Mike could complete his maneuver, I flipped the hitch ball sack with my wrist and jabbed my hand forward, catching, and momentarily pinning his knife hand, while stepping into position and delivering a side kick. My heel caught Mike's good leg, right at the top of the kneecap. He went down again, and I raised the hitch ball sack up for a backhand swing aimed at his head. The blow caught him in the face and forehead. I thought I heard bone crunch, and sensed the force of the impact. He dropped in an awkward sprawl. His leg quivered a moment, then he lay still. Mike's clean-up fight was over.

I turned toward Gary again, he was struggling to sit up, but not able to recover well. I straightened and backed up a few steps, heaving a sigh of relief and letting my heart rate begin to normalize.

"You can sit there a minute," I said to Gary. "But don't get stupid."

He looked at me with unfocused eyes, barely able to sit erect. After a few minutes, my breathing was normal, and I had figured out what I was going to do next. Gary was looking as though he could see straight again, but he flinched with any little movement. I walked over, pulled one of his legs out from under him and toppled him to the ground again. Then, holding his foot twisted enough I could inflict whatever pain I needed to keep him on his belly, I undid his shoelace. I tucked the end of the lace under my belt, dropped his foot and repeated the process with the other leg.

When I was done, I told him to sit back up again, with his legs tucked under him. It obviously wasn't easy, but he managed it. Once he had settled into a sitting position, I used one of the shoelaces to tie his thumbs together, with his hands behind his back. Then I helped him to his feet and led him over to Mike's pickup, told him to lean across the tailgate as far as he could, then grabbed his ankles and heaved him up onto the bed of the pickup. As a final measure, I pulled his shoes off and tied his big toes together behind him with the rest of the shoelace, effectively hog-tying him.

Mike was a little harder to deal with, in that he was still unconscious. I checked, and he was breathing, so I wrestled him onto the tailgate the hard way—lifting his body myself—then shoved him forward so I could close the tailgate. Just for insurance, I tied his hands behind his back similar to the way I had secured Gary. He started waking up as I finished.

As I closed the tailgate, Gary called out in panic. "What the hell you doing?"

"Don't worry," I said. "I'll send someone for you. Just chill out." Then, I took the keys out of the pickup and locked everything up with Gary and Mike inside, demanding to be let out.

CHAPTER FIFTY-TWO

I WAS SORE from where Mike had kicked me in the midsection, but not broken up inside. The cut he had given me left my shirt bloody and my belly sore as hell, but I didn't think the cut was too deep. I folded a bandana and stuck the makeshift bandage to my belly with duct tape. Always carry duct tape.

Put together as best as I could hope for at the moment, I wiped the seat of my motorcycle off with my hand—as a symbolic gesture against Gary having ridden the bike without my permission, not because it was actually dirty—and climbed on. I didn't know where I was, but felt confident I could figure it out after a while. Being a little lost was a lot better than being in the back of Mike's pickup, waiting for him to do his thing. I drank in the smell of the pines, and enjoyed the feel of the wind combing my hair as I drove down the road in the direction Gary had come with my bike.

I found my way back into town, making note of the route I had taken so I could tell Lucinda where the police could find the pickup, and drove to the police station. Luckily, Lucinda was in. Although wanting to hear about my fight with Mike and Gary, she got freaked out by the blood all over my shirt, and insisted on taking me to the emergency room to have the cut taken care of. It didn't take long, this time, and there were no threats about keeping me there. So far, so good.

Since we were already at the hospital, it made sense to check in on Teresa. The hallway was clean, antiseptic and sterile. Noises suggested some of the patients were watching television. A blinking red light signaled someone's desire for a nurse's attention. The light flooding Teresa's room from windows with shades pulled back seemed a declaration of someone on the mend, and not in critical condition. Teresa lay half upright in her bed under a taut white sheet pulled against her waist. Her white hospital gown looked fresh, and someone had brushed her shiny black hair. Her face lit up with a bright smile when we walked into the room. She told us her parents had just left, and asked if we had seen them in the hallway or elevator. I explained that we had come up the stairs, and had not run into anyone.

"Oh," she said. "That's too bad. I'd like them to meet you."

"Maybe next time," Lucinda said.

The bruises on the side of Teresa's face, and the way her lips seemed unwilling to move on that side of her mouth, suggested the smile she had managed when she first saw us had come at some cost.

"How you making out, Sweetie?" Lucinda said.

I walked over to the bed and took Teresa's hand in both of mine, just holding her, afraid to squeeze too hard, but not wanting to let her go. She looked up at me, eyes alight.

"I'm doing pretty well," she said.

When Lucinda asked her about the hit-and-run, she said she was walking home, and was hit crossing a side street.

"Did you see the driver, or the vehicle?" Lucinda asked.

"Not really," Teresa aid. "But I know who did it."

"How do you know who did it, if you didn't see them?" Lucinda said.

Teresa explained that she had been confronted by Mike before she left the church. She glanced at me. "It wasn't about making nasty gestures, this time," she said.

"What was it about?" I asked.

She took a deep breath before launching into her story.

Teresa said she had met Sheri at the church the day Sheri was murdered. Sheri had said her parents, the Nortons, had been arguing that morning about a necklace Mr. Norton had given his wife, and the fact that she hadn't been wearing it. Without letting Mr. Norton know about it, Mrs. Norton sent Sheri to the church to run an errand for her, and concocted a story for her husband about needing her sweater and not having time to get it herself. Actually, Sheri was to look for the missing necklace as well.

Teresa looked embarrassed and tucked her head.

"Mrs. Norton was having an affair with Pastor Martin," she said. "That's why she thought her necklace was at the church. It must have come off when they were together."

"Sheri found it, and the sweater she was supposed to pick up. She put the necklace on herself. We were in the robing room, talking about everything that was going on, and we heard kind of a commotion in the hallway," Teresa said. "Ben Edwards, the choir director, and Mrs. MacDonald one of the women in the

Ladies Aid Group, were talking with Deacon Thomas—saying they wanted to use his office."

Teresa stopped for a minute, looking awkward. Lucinda gently prodded her to continue.

"Well, this is all kind of embarrassing," Teresa said. "I mean, we knew what they wanted to use the office for. So did Deacon Thomas, and he wasn't very happy. I can't blame him."

"Are you trying to say Ben Edwards and Mrs. MacDonald wanted to use the office to have sex?" Lucinda said.

Teresa nodded her head in reply. "They finally got their way, and Deacon Thomas came into the robing room to wait until they finished. He didn't know we were there. We were sort of hidden in back of the robes. I told Sheri we should sneak out, but she wouldn't come with me. She just shook her head and made it clear she wanted to watch what was going on. We could hear Mr. Edwards and Mrs. MacDonald starting to go at it. Finally, I snuck out and left without anybody hearing me."

"And Sheri stayed?" Lucinda said.

Teresa nodded again in confirmation.

"Then, after I was home," Teresa said, "I started feeling really guilty about leaving Sheri there, so I went back. I was home quite a while, so I didn't know if she'd still be there by the time I could get back, but I had to try. When I got to church, somebody was leaving in a car that I'm sure was Ernesto's, the man who's in jail for murdering Sheri. Actually, there were two men, but I didn't get a look at their faces. I know one of them was Gary, because he was big and had red hair."

Teresa paused and took a breath.

"Mike was right behind them," she said. Her voice started to quiver. Lucinda patted her arm to sooth her and urge her to continue.

"He had the sweater Sheri was sent after. He was holding it in his fist, outside his window. It looked like he was shaking it at the men in the car, but when he saw me, he pulled his hand in and threw the sweater on the seat. Then, he looked at me and pointed his hand right at my face, you know, like he was shooting a pistol. I got scared. I ran inside and looked for Sheri, but nobody was around. I didn't look long, though. Like I said, I got scared."

"What did you do when you stopped looking for Sheri?" Lucinda asked.

"I ran home again, before Mike could come back and find me still there."

"And, you're sure it was the sweater belonging to Mrs. Norton that Sheri had been sent after?"

"It looked just like it. I mean, it was the same color, and everything. It wasn't a man's sweater, that's for sure. Not anything Mike would wear."

Lucinda looked at me as she asked Teresa her next question. "How about the necklace?"

Teresa shook her head. "I told you, Sheri put it on herself," she said.

"Did Mike ever talk to you about the event? Warn you against telling anyone?" Lucinda asked.

Teresa nodded again. "He told me to keep my mouth shut about anything that wasn't my business. I knew he meant it, too. He's really scary."

"Why didn't you tell anyone about this before?" Lucinda asked.

"I was too scared."

Teresa turned to look at me. "I've been scared the whole time. Ever since it happened. I just wanted to get away, like climb on a motorcycle like yours and drive away and never come back," she said.

She looked back at Lucinda. "Then, the night I was hit, Mike was standing outside in the parking lot. He made a gesture for me to come over to him, but I was too scared. I just pretended I didn't see him, and kept walking. So, I know it was him. I even heard his truck coming down the street after me. I tried to run, but I wasn't fast enough. Then, I woke up in here."

CHAPTER FIFTY-THREE

LUCINDA AND I went back to the station, and I made out a statement about what had happened to me, starting with getting hit from behind in the parking lot of the supermarket, and ending with my stuffing Gary and Mike into the back of Mike's pickup. Mike and Gary had been picked up and brought to the hospital as well. It turned out neither had crushed skulls from my slamming them with the hitch ball sack—too bad, in a way. Needless to say, we didn't drop in to pay them a visit after we saw Teresa.

The next couple of days were long and difficult. Long, because I had nothing to do. Difficult, because Gary and Mike weren't talking, Ben had lawyered up, and both Pastor Martin and Deacon Thomas were being left to shiver and sweat while the wheels of justice did their slow grind. Of course, I stayed in close touch with Lucinda. On the second day, Lucinda even bought me lunch.

"Light at the end of the tunnel," she said. She grinned as she peered over her chicken salad sandwich. I was having a Rueben.

"Gary finally decided to buy himself a little slack by cooperating," she said. "Gary knows he'll do time, but wants to lessen the penalty as much as he can. What he's saying, is that Mike did the killing when it came to shutting Daryl up, and Mike called the shots as far as the attempt on your life. Gary claims he didn't even know about the hit-and-run on Teresa, but told us Mike said he was going to 'take care of her personally'."

"That's fantastic," I said. I dunked a fry into a puddle of catsup and popped it into my mouth.

Lucinda continued the update.

"We brought Deacon Thomas in," she said. "He's been sitting in the interview room for a couple of hours. I think he might like a little company, after we finish lunch. We'll pay him a visit."

"Think he'll say anything?" I asked.

"Let's hope so," she said. "I talked to Chief Mac-Donald, and he's agreed to let you listen in from the other side of the glass, since you've been helping us out so much. This way, if he says something off base that triggers more of your own recollections, you'll be able to get word to whoever is interviewing him at the time, and we can use it to put pressure on him to tell us the truth."

I was eager to finish lunch and get right to the station. Lucinda insisted we take our time.

"Let him feel some heat and think things over," she said. "He was pretty cocky when he was first brought in. I'm sure he has rehearsed the story he plans to tell, and has convinced himself he has it down pat. Sitting and waiting a while will eat away at some of that confidence. He'll think about what others may have said, and begin to think his own story sounds less solid. That's when he might decide to make the right decisions about what he says when he talks to us.

After what seemed like hours, but wasn't, Lucinda picked up the tab and I followed her to the police station. She quickly checked a couple of messages at her desk that had come in while she was out, and then led me to a small room next to the interview room. Inside, there were four metal chairs lined up facing the two-way mirror. Detective Alvarez sat in the near chair, holding a clipboard with a notepad on it. He nodded, first at Lucinda, then at me, as we entered. I almost expected him to tell me to go in the other room and sit down at the interview table. Of course, he didn't. He actually seemed pleasant.

This time, the person sitting in the hot seat at the metal table, trying to look composed and not accomplishing it—was Deacon Thomas. He straightened a little in his chair when Detective Alvarez went in. His lower lip trembled and I didn't know if he was about to start crying, or was just showing his nervousness.

"Do you understand why we are talking today Mr. Hansen?" Detective Alvarez asked Deacon Thomas.

Deacon Thomas made a brief gesture with his hands, lifted his eyebrows and took a deep breath. "I know a lot of things have happened recently," he said. "But, I'm not sure how they're supposed to involve me at all."

The faint lisp made his statement sound affected, somehow, but then, that was part of his personality, too.

Lucinda looked at him—with a patient, somewhat amused expression.

"Would you prefer I call you Deacon Thomas, Mr. Hansen? I understand most people do."

"Deacon Thomas is fine," he said.

"Well, Deacon Thomas, what you just told me is not entirely true," Detective Alvarez said. "Of course, you're probably not sure how much we know. Unfortunately for you, we know a lot."

Detective Alvarez let him think that over a couple of minutes.

"Deacon Thomas, who killed Sheri Norton?"

"What...? I don't know... how would I know that? Why are you even asking me?"

"Because we know you did it, Deacon Thomas. Why don't you do the right thing—the Christian thing—and tell us what happened?"

"What do you mean? Why are you blaming me?" Deacon Thomas' voice was shaky, his eyes wide with fright.

"Someone has come forward and told us what happened. We'd like you to tell us your side of the story, Deacon Thomas."

Detective Alvarez paused, then continued in a soft, reassuring voice. "We're not trying to say you meant to do it. Just tell us how it happened, what went wrong, and how she came to die. Then, we can put this to rest and be finished here."

"I didn't do anything. Whoever told you I did?" Deacon Thomas said. He was staring hard at Detective Alvarez, appearing earnest and intent, trying hard as hell, I thought, to convince him of his innocence. Only thing was, he had to clinch his hands into fists and press them against the tabletop, because they shook too much otherwise. His leg was trembling violently too; I guess he hoped it wouldn't be too noticeable underneath the table.

"Right now, who told us you killed her is not your biggest concern. We do have someone who told us, though. Said you killed her at the church."

Deacon Thomas' eyes flew wide open, and his head jerked in realization who the likely informant would be, one of those involved in cleaning up afterward—Mike or Gary.

"Let me put this a different way, Deacon Thomas, were you at the church the morning Sheri was killed?"

Deacon Thomas hesitated so long, Detective Alvarez had to prod him. "Were you?" he said.

Deacon Thomas nodded his head slowly. "Yes," he said. "I'm there every day. I'm always there."

"Did you leave the church, for any reason, in the late morning?" Detective Alvarez asked.

"No. I never left the church until late afternoon. The same as I always do."

The cockiness had returned somewhat. Deacon Thomas sat up, prim and proper, and smirked at Detective Alvarez. "There are others who will remember my being there, too," he said. "They can vouch for me. I'm sure Pastor Martin will tell you I was there all afternoon.

"So, I assume that will that be all you need me for," Deacon Thomas said. He started to stand up.

"Sit down and shut up," Detective Alvarez said. He stood up and walked out of the interview room. Moments later, the door to the little side room opened, and Detective Alvarez entered, holding a recorder.

"Hey, Lucinda, I've got something you need to listen to," he said. "I knew there was something familiar about that guy. It finally came to me. When I was investigating the scene when Sheri Norton's body was found by Bobby, here, someone called 911. The caller wouldn't give a name, but said the person who had been the driver of the car had left and later returned to the scene on a motorcycle. He had a little speech impediment."

He turned the machine on. We listened to the dispatcher's voice begin the 911 response.

"What is your emergency, sir?"

"Well, something is going on across the street from where I'm at, and I might have some information that could be of help"

The voice was unmistakable. I strained to listen, fascinated at what I was hearing.

"What information would that be, sir?" the dispatcher said.

"The officers are talking with a man right now... he's acting like he just came along on his motorcycle, and found something awful in the trunk of the car. But... I saw him earlier—without the motorcycle. He was the one driving the car they're all looking at. He left it there and went away. Now he's back."

I looked at Lucinda to see if her reaction was the same as mine.

"Well, isn't that handy? Somebody was trying to be clever, wasn't he?" she said.

The lisp and haughty attitude were unmistakable. "Deacon Thomas called in the 911 on me," I said. "It wasn't the old geezer, after all."

Detective Alvarez sat up straight, a smile spread across his face. "Thought you might like to hear that before I go back in," he said.

"You said you never left the church, Deacon Thomas. Clearly, you did," Detective Alvarez said. "You need to tell me why you made the 911 call."

Deacon Thomas' shoulders slumped. He dropped his head forward and spread his fingers on the tabletop, as though trying to grasp stability from the cold, unyielding surface. Then he answered, his voice lowered, and carrying in it a sound of resignation.

"I had the idea that it would be a good thing to involve someone else, spread the suspicion around a bit. Ernesto, leaving that car of his where we could take it, had been a handy gift from above; maybe the motorcyclist would be another."

"But, why were you there?" Detective Alvarez asked.

"They made me drive the car. Mike and Gary. We left it there, and walked away. Mike was supposed to pick us both up at the end of the block, but he just took Gary. I asked what they were doing, but they flipped me off and told me to walk. The bastards!"

He finished by banging his fist on the table. "But I didn't kill anyone," he said.

"Then, you'd better tell us who did," Detective Alvarez said.

Deacon Thomas' mouth twisted into a toothed, snarling orifice. His eyebrows knotted like a hemp rope. "It was Ben Edwards," he said with a guttural explosion. "Our wonderful choir director raped her, and killed her afterwards."

CHAPTER FIFTY-FOUR

DARYL THOUGHT HIS half-brother Ben was guilty of Betsy's murder, and must have been guilty of Sheri's, too. Now, Deacon Thomas was pointing the finger at Ben as well. Detective Alvarez, Lucinda and I were sitting around his desk, going over Deacon Thomas' statement, and talking over the case in general. Deacon Thomas had been left to sweat some more in the interview room.

"The part I'm having trouble with, is why Deacon Thomas would be forced to drive the car as part of the clean-up crew. Gary and Mike could have handled that alone," Detective Alvarez said.

"I think he's still lying," Lucinda said. "He's still trying to throw as much blame as he can on someone else."

Detective Alvarez agreed. I thought about my encounters with Deacon Thomas at the Holiness Pentecostal Church of the Brethren, my times with Daryl, and the event that brought me into the picture in the first place, finding Sheri's body in the trunk of Ernesto's car. I remembered the marks on her neck, the bruising. There were heavy marks, like something made by hands gripping her throat in a strangulating hold. But, I remembered another set of marks as well—a ligature mark, a thin bruise line in addition to the heavier bruises.

"Was Mrs. Norton's necklace ever found?" I asked.

"What? Where did that question come from?" Lucinda said.

"I've just been going over everything," I said. "Sheri Norton went to the church to pick up her mother's sweater. Her real mission was to find her mother's lost necklace while she was at it."

"Yes... so?" Lucinda said.

"Teresa told us Sheri found it, and put it on," I said. "Teresa said Mike was waving the sweater at the people driving Ernesto's car, then tossed it on the seat inside his own pickup when he realized she was looking at them."

"Right."

"What happened to the sweater and necklace?" I said.

Lucinda shook her head. "Don't know," she said. "He probably dumped that stuff somewhere. We may never find out, if no one opens up."

"I have a funny hunch I may know what happened to that necklace," I said.

Detective Alvarez started. "You do?"

I told them about the necklace Gary and I found hung up in the leg of one of the tables the first night I helped set up for the Bible study group.

"That had to be it." I said. "The thing is, Gary didn't react at all when we found it. The two people who did... were Pastor Martin and Deacon Thomas. Deacon Thomas was dead set on us giving it to him. Pastor Martin intervened and insisted on taking it instead. He said he would get it back to the rightful owner. I think he knew Mrs. Norton had lost it when they were making out. When it turned up later, he knew exactly who it belonged to. Deacon Thomas knew something too. He knew Sheri had been wearing it when she was raped and killed."

CHAPTER FIFTY-FIVE

LUCINDA HAD REPLACED Detective Alvarez when we all went back to continue the interview. He and I were watching through the two-way mirror in the adjacent room. Lucinda entered and sat opposite Deacon Thomas at the metal table, then took a couple of minutes, to shuffle through some papers.

"Mr. Hanson, you told us Ben Edwards was responsible for Sheri's death," she said.

Deacon Thomas leaned forward, eagerly. "You're surprised, aren't you?" he said. "Everyone thinks Ben is so good, but I see the other side of him—who he really is."

Lucinda was sitting at the table opposite Deacon Thomas. She leaned back against her chair, looking calm—relaxed even.

"Ben admits he was there, at the church. But, he has a very different account from yours about what took place. And, he has someone to corroborate his version. Actually, there is more than one person to corroborate Ben Edward's account. Now, would you like to tell us what really happened? Because, we know you did it."

Deacon Thomas looked stunned, his face as pale as if he had no blood left in his veins at all. His eyes bugged out a little. His hand no longer trembled against the top of the table. He just sat, motionless.

"Remember the first night Bobby Navarro helped set up for the Bible Study meeting?" Lucinda said.

Deacon Thomas looked at her, confused and startled by the new direction the interview was taking.

"Remember that whole thing about a necklace he and Gary found jammed into the folding mechanism of one of the tables when you were all cleaning up after the meeting?" Lucinda said.

Deacon Thomas tensed, alert and suspicious.

"You were quite eager to get that necklace. You knew Sheri Norton was wearing it when you raped her. The necklace places Sheri at the church when she was murdered, wouldn't you say? But, Pastor Martin recognized it as one Mrs. Norton was wearing when they were together, and ended up taking it from you, so he could return it to Mrs. Norton."

Deacon Thomas stared at Lucinda, like a field mouse hypnotized by a rattlesnake.

"You broke the chain when you raped, and then strangled her, didn't you, Deacon Thomas? Sheri's mother had lost it at the church. Sheri was sent to get it. But, it got lost again, thrown aside, like her clothes. It got stuck in the table leg. Remember? When you saw it, you realized it might be evidence against you. It is evidence against you, and not Ben Edwards. He didn't know who it belonged to, and wasn't interested in getting ahold of it. You were."

Lucinda paused for a minute, letting the implication of her statement sink in.

"Tell us what happened, Deacon Thomas. It's all coming out now, one way or another."

When Deacon Thomas finally spoke, his voice was soft, pleading, almost childlike.

"Do you have to hear about *everything*?"

"Yes. I do," Lucinda said.

Deacon Thomas sat in a frozen lump for another half minute, or so, then whatever fighting energy he had remaining seeped away.

"Ben Edwards came into the office with Cathy MacDonald, the organist, and he demanded they have use of the office. Ben was all hot and bothered. He told me I'd just have to get out. She did too. They couldn't wait to get at each other."

He tensed up again.

"They both just assumed they could come in there and kick me out so they could do their thing."

After a pause, Lucinda urged him along. "So... you left them... closed the door behind you... and did what?"

"I *slammed* it closed. But, you could still *hear* everything clearly enough."

"Where did you wait all that time?"

Deacon Thomas turned his head to the side, clenched his hands into little fists again, and then looked at her as he growled his answer. "I was in the robing area. I mean, why should I leave altogether? Why should I have to get out just for them?"

"I can appreciate your feelings, Deacon Thomas. So, what happened next?"

Deacon Thomas hesitated a long time, longer than before. When he spoke, he sat like a wooden mannequin, and told his story in a flat voice.

"I was in the robing area. Because... like I told you... why should I do everything to get out of *their* way? I mean, you could hear everything plain, as if you were watching a porno flick, or something."

He snuck a glance at her at his mention of porno flicks, but Lucinda didn't respond, and he turned his gaze back into the distance and went on.

"Well, it... got to be a turn-on. Listening to them. You know? Picturing what they were doing? Because, they were talking about it all the time. You know, taking each other's clothes off, slobbering over each other. You could tell what she was doing to *him*, because she talked about how good it looked, then how good it tasted. After a while, I had to do something."

Deacon Thomas paused.

"Go on," Lucinda said.

"Like I said, I had to do *something*, so I unzipped and took my stuff out. Most of the robes are real silky, you know. You can smell the perfume on some of them. I just wanted to feel that silkiness... when I took care of my own needs."

Deacon Thomas took a deep breath.

"It turned out, Sheri was there, too. In the robing room. She saw me. I didn't realize she was there when I went in. Maybe she came in after I did. I'm not sure. Anyway, we could both hear *them* going at it. Cathy can get pretty loud."

"What happened next?"

"At first, when I realized Sheri was watching me, I was afraid she was going to scream, or make fun of me or something. Because, she said, 'Oh, what happened to it? Did I scare it away?'

"I got really embarrassed. But that's not what she meant. I mean, she wasn't trying to embarrass me.... more like... she liked seeing it the way it was before."

I could see Lucinda tense up at his suggestion of Sheri *liking* it. Deacon Thomas hesitated, with his head tilted up a little, like he was trying to look back into that moment when Sheri had caught him.

"She asked if I'd like her to help me get back up. Like she *wanted* to do it. Not like she was teasing me. Girls have sometimes, you know—teased me. They act like they don't think I'm... man enough for them."

"Did you let her?"

Deacon Thomas nodded.

"Her hand was so soft, and it felt good. Then I wanted more. I knew she did too. So, I grabbed her and kissed her, and she didn't yell at me to stop, or pull away, or anything. She kissed me back. And, when I pulled her down and started ripping her clothes off, she just moaned and laid there."

"What went wrong?" Lucinda said.

His voice caught, and his nose was running. He pulled out a handkerchief and wiped at it, then blew.

"I guess it hurt her a little—and she wanted me to stop," he said.

"Did you stop?"

Deacon Thomas' head pivoted slowly from side to side and the words tumbled out with a flow of tears and shaggy breaths of air.

"I couldn't. I didn't mean to hurt her though."

Deacon Thomas finished his account with some additional coaxing from Lucinda. He told us he had clamped his hand over Sheri's mouth and nose to stifle her cries for him to stop, and then harder when she tried to cry for help. When he was finished, he found she was no longer struggling—or breathing. Realizing the couple in the office would be coming out soon, he dragged Sheri's body to the corner of the room and threw her clothes and one of the robes over it, hoping no one would notice.

After Ben and Cathy left, first telling him he could go back and use the office, he checked to see if anyone was outside in the parking lot. Ernesto's car was there, but Ernesto himself was not around. Mike saw him and demanded to know what the hell he was up to. When he couldn't answer, Mike shoved him back into the church and checked the rooms to see what might have been going on. He found Sheri's body, and that was enough to kick in his marching orders.

Mike and Gary carried Sheri's body outside, wrapped in a choir robe, and put it in the trunk of the car, keeping the robe. Mike wadded it up, told Deacon Thomas to get rid of it, and to keep his fucking mouth shut. Deacon Thomas disposed of the robe and Sheri's clothes in a plastic bag that he stuffed into the garbage. He got lucky when it was picked up before anyone knew Sheri's death was in any way connected with the church. For the rest, Deacon Thomas just prayed the whole incident would go away. He prayed even more fervently that Mike would not do something to make him pay for their inconvenience. As we soon learned, it was a repeat inconvenience.

"What about Betsy Horvath?" Lucinda asked.

Deacon Thomas seemed to have been expecting Lucinda to ask about Betsy at some point. He answered readily, and without any attempt to point a finger elsewhere this time. He admitted killing her under similar circumstances. In Betsy's case, no one had come in and demanded the use of the office for their own sexual pleasure. His account was that Betsy's death, like Sheri's had been unintended, an attempt to quiet a girl from screaming her accusations to others. Mike had cleaned up that affair, as well. It was part of the reason Tom feared

Mike's reaction to the latest need for someone to sanitize the scene.

I think Deacon Thomas had been harboring more fear of Mike's reactions than those of the police. With the police, he'd get a trial, and he would be put in jail. Mike would simply kill him, and not necessarily in any way that reflected a humanitarian concern, or drew any distinction between simple murder and various ways Mike knew to make death seem like a favor.

He might have had good reason for his concerns, too. Since Mike was in a mood to clean house, I'm sure he would have gotten around to Deacon Thomas before long. Deacon Thomas could have ended up in yet another "accident". But he didn't. Because Ben thought Daryl had killed Betsy Horvath, and made him help hide the body. Ben got away with it, at the time, because Daryl thought the police would blame him for her death, if he said anything, and he was probably right. They did blame him, for a while. Then they found another suspect easier to prosecute and put him in prison. That was Betsy Horvath's murder. The first murder victim.

Then, of course, I happened to hear some nitwit bang into Ernesto's car, and discovered Sheri Norton's body. After that, I sat down next to Daryl at breakfast. And, he was horrified because he thought his half-brother had raped and killed again, and he wanted Ben to stop, and to be made to pay for what he had done. So, he blurted out that he knew who killed Sheri, and I heard him say it. I told Lucinda what I'd heard, because I knew her back when. Next thing, I was involved in Sheri Norton's murder investigation.

Unfortunately, Mike and Gary killed Daryl, because Mike thought Daryl had talked too much. And, I guess he had. He had talked too much to me, and I wouldn't let go.

Because I couldn't get the face of a dead girl out of my head.

Or turn down a request for help from a very pretty cop I once knew in high school.

Or just walk away from whatever was taking the lives of young women at the Holiness Pentecostal Church of the Brethren.

CHAPTER FIFTY-SIX

THE POLICE HELD Mike and Gary for arraignment for their role in cleaning-up after the murders of both girls, their murder of Daryl and their attempt on me. Ben was released, pending further consideration by the District Attorney's office. Since he was Daryl's next of kin, it fell to him to decide how Daryl's body would be handled. Ben decided to have him buried in a plot next to Daryl's own mother. He didn't want anything elaborate, but the mortician talked him into a simple service at the mortuary chapel. There weren't many people in attendance, but I guess the word got out to a few. Amanda Trainer, the woman who sometimes played the organ at church, was one of them. Lucinda and I were there as well.

Like Sheri Norton, and Betsy Horvath, Daryl's death had been a life cut short. Only, in Daryl's case, there wasn't a congregation of church members to honor him on his way, just a few people he'd touched more than he probably realized. The mortician didn't try to go on about Daryl's life, or eulogize him in any way. It was just a simple matter of turning over his soul to its assumed next phase of whatever awaited.

Amanda dabbed at her eyes with a handkerchief during the brief ceremony. Lucinda was calm and respectful, but I doubt she had very strong emotional feelings about Daryl, except to realize he came through at the end. I was glad she was there, never-theless. For myself, I felt a sense of both loss and frustration. Well, I felt guilt, too. I can't say Daryl and I had become best buddies, but he wasn't all that bad, and I still felt responsible for his death. I told myself, his death had everything to do with trying to make things right for Betsy. But, when someone gets killed for doing the right thing—and you're involved—you feel responsible. I think I was, at least partially.

Daryl had it pretty tough, as a kid. That's the part I'll think about the most, his life growing up, feeling he wasn't wanted. Kids shouldn't have to grow up that way. I wondered if he felt responsible for the confus-ing relationship he had with the man and the family that took him in. Kids often do. Ben could have been a big help, if he had been the big brother Daryl needed. Too bad it didn't work out that way. I hate it when kids don't get the chance for a decent life.

Lucinda had invited me to join her and Miguella for another meal after the service for Daryl. I followed her on my motorcycle to their home.

"Miguella is with the woman who takes care of her for me when I have to work," she said. "We can sit and have a glass of wine for a little while. We're hav-ing steak, so dinner won't take long."

She let out a deep sigh and smiled at me. "Would you rather have a beer?"

I told her a beer sounded good, and she said I should make myself comfortable in the living room. I'd been in her home before, but I looked around again at the furniture, all matching, in a worn-but-still-nice, southwestern style. A nice print of an adobe church, or mission, hung on the wall opening to the kitchen. A larger print of open country with Saguaro cacti and sage dotting the landscape, and bluish hills fading into the distance hung on the wall opposite. It felt comfortable, and homey. I sat down on the couch.

"Well, we did it," Lucinda said when she came back into the living room. "It didn't turn out quite the way I thought it would, but we found out who killed Sheri Norton, and who actually killed Betsy Horvath, thanks to all your good work."

"I assume Ernesto will be released, now," I said.

"I'm sure he will, and the fellow in prison for Betsy Horvath's death, as well," Lucinda said.

She handed me a tall beer bottle, already opened. "I didn't think you'd want it in a glass."

"This is just fine," I said.

She sat down on the couch alongside me, but not overly close. A sudden gust of air blew in through the door opened to her patio out back. It smelled of ozone, and a promise of rain. The sky hadn't looked that threatening on the drive over. I doubted it would amount to much, but in the southwest, rain always carries some anticipation.

"I suppose Ben's going to have to answer for stealing Betsy's body," I said.

"He will, but I doubt the court will be that harsh. He was smart to give us the location of her burial. That will help his case. He has a good reputation in the community, as far as that goes," she said. "I wouldn't be surprised if he gets off without doing any jail time at all. Same with Pastor Martin. Ultimately, and morally, he was at the top of the heap, and bears responsibility for everything that went on at the church, and with the church congregation. At the same time, Mike was the heavy in this case, and I suspect that Pastor Martin will get off without having to pay the Piper.

Suddenly, the front door burst open, and Miguella scurried into the room. The woman I assumed to have been taking care of her followed. Lucinda introduced us. I stood up and said I was glad to meet her. She waved at me from across the room.

"I have to get right back," the woman said. "Our little angel had a lovely time helping me sort out some pieces for a quilt I'm starting. She was very helpful."

The woman beamed down at Miguella, then told me what a pleasure it had been to meet me, gave a kiss and hug to Miguella, blew another kiss to Lucinda, and let herself back out.

"Mommy, she's making a very special quilt," Miguella said. "I can't tell you who it's going to be for, because it will be a surprise, but it's going to be soooo beautiful!"

Lucinda laughed. "Aren't you forgetting to greet our guest, and welcome him to our home?"

Miguella threw a startled look at me, then came over to where I still stood and threw her arms around my legs and hugged me. When she released me, she looked up and told me she was sorry she hadn't told me right away how nice it was to see me. Of course, she had me the second she gave me the hug.

Lucinda sent Miguella to her room to put away the things brought back by her babysitter. When Miguella returned, Lucinda offered her some juice to drink.

"Can I have a glass just like yours, Mommy?"

Lucinda laughed and said wine glasses were for grownups. She poured Miguella her juice, and we all sat down again.

"Are we having a party?" Miguella asked.

"Well, something like that," Lucinda said. "Bobby is joining us for dinner tonight. We're kind of celebrating all he has done to help Mommy with her work, and the fact that together we stopped some bad people from hurting others."

"Oh," Miguella said. "Then, we should have cake for dessert, too."

We both laughed at that, and Lucinda turned toward me and clinked her glass against my bottle. Miguella carefully squirmed her way off her chair and came over to clink her juice glass against ours.

"I really do owe you a debt of gratitude for all you did," Lucinda said to me.

"I'm glad it turned out so well. I wasn't so sure it would, for a while."

We chatted, with Miguella telling us all about her day at her sitter's. After a while, Lucinda announced that she was going to make a salad for dinner. She said Miguella could help her. They had barely made it into the kitchen, when Miguella whirled around and came back. She cupped her free hand around her mouth and spoke in a loud, stage whisper. "Are you going to be Mommy's boyfriend?"

I laughed out loud, and heard Lucinda's scolding reminder that such questions of guests were not polite.

"Your mommy and I are friends," I said. "We have known each other for a very long time. Since we were in high school, before you were born."

Miguella stared at me with saucer-sized eyes that were going to make some lucky man fall in love with her the first time he saw her. I couldn't tell if the wide-eyed looked was her reaction to the idea that her mother and I could ever have been young enough to be in school, or that I could possibly have fit into her mother's life before she even came along. Then, apparently satisfied by my explanation of my standing, she threw me a happy smile and spun back in her original direction and joined her mother in the kitchen.

CHAPTER FIFTY-SEVEN

IN THE MORNING, I packed my bike to head out. I decided to have breakfast at the diner before I left town. I was surprised to see Rudy, the mountain man, sitting down at the end of the counter. I also felt glad to run into him before leaving.

"From all the news I've been hearing, I gather a lot has happened. I have a feeling it involved you—in no small way perhaps."

"How you doing, Rudy?" I said.

I sat down and ordered. The waitress was Carrie again, and seeing her made everything feel all the more familiar.

"I take it you have completed your quest," Rudy said.

"I guess you can say that."

"Too bad about our friend, Daryl, though," he said.

I couldn't have agreed more.

"And, how are you faring?" he asked.

I shrugged. "I'm okay."

He studied me in silence for a minute.

"One's feelings aren't always easy to deal with. They are important, though."

"I hear that's what makes us human," I said.

He assumed a calm, patient expression.

"I believe we humans are not the only creatures under the sun and moon to have feelings," he said.

"In fact, I know this to be the case from my observations of them. No offense intended."

"None taken. Actually, I agree."

"So where have your feelings brought you at the moment?" he asked.

I thanked Carrie for the mug of coffee she had placed on the countertop in front of me.

"I can't say I feel as good as I'd like to, now that this thing is getting wrapped up. I mean, I'm glad it is, but it still doesn't make everything okay again."

He nodded, but didn't interrupt with any comment.

I felt I was expected to continue. I did.

"I guess it provides something of a sense of closure for Betsy's parents. Sheri's, too. I suppose that's something. It cost Daryl his life, though. That part pisses me off," I said.

Rudy nodded again.

"But, now no other girls will have go through what happened to Sheri and Betsy."

"An important point, indeed," Rudy said.

My own thoughts went on to Teresa Gonzales. Now, she should be safe to grow up. That felt good.

Rudy didn't ask me to go over all the details of everything that had happened from my own vantage point, and I appreciated that he didn't. All he said was, "And, now you have to integrate everything that was a part of your quest into your own life—as you lead your life forward. Bear in mind, that may take some time," he said.

Carrie placed a platter of huevos rancheros in front of me. I thanked her, and picked up a fork. I knew Rudy was right. I'd have to deal with Daryl's murder, and my experiences with the Holiness Pentecostal

Church of the Brethren, and the murders, in the days and months ahead. I wasn't sure what that would amount to, and assumed I would just have to let it happen as time did its thing.

I ate my breakfast. Rudy finished his coffee. We talked a little, but not much. When he got up to leave, Carrie brought my check.

"I guess you're going to be leaving us soon. Isn't that right, Lover?" she said.

"Afraid so," I said. I smiled at her and gave her the money for my meal.

CHAPTER FIFTY-EIGHT

THE WIND SLAPPING against my face carried a strong scent of pine as the Ponderosas slipped by on either side of the highway heading east on Forty. The sky was deep and blue overhead, and the sun shone down from the peak of its trek across the heavens. The exhaust pipes of my Harley left a throaty serenade behind me as I laid down the miles, and as the road ahead unfolded in an open invitation to whatever might be waiting. I felt good to be on the road, but also sad about things I was leaving behind.

Rudy had pointed out that I hadn't come into to town until after Sheri Norton was killed; there was no way I could have saved her. He said that wasn't what I was meant to be there for, and I had done what I *was* meant to do. I stopped because of a minor fender bender, and found Sheri's body in the trunk of Ernesto's car. I followed up on Daryl's rants and ramblings, and the trail led to solving Sheri's murder, as well as Betsy Horvath's, and uncovering the mystery of Betsy's disappearance. What more could I have asked for? Well, the growing emptiness inside me suggested I wanted to ask for something more, but I wasn't sure I could say what it was.

I knew Lucinda and Miguella figured into my mixed feelings about leaving. Of course, I knew they would be fine. And, they left me with an open invitation to come back. I told them I'd like to do that.

For me, the two of them represented family, something I didn't have. Never had had. Something I thought would be really nice. Trouble is, sometimes the hardest thing to do is to take a chance on the things you want most. Sometimes people who go through divorce are gun-shy at the thought of marriage. I haven't ever been divorced, myself. With me, the fear is wanting a family, telling myself I finally have one, and then risk losing them—for whatever reason. It makes me afraid to take a chance, although I really wish I could.

According to Rudy, the whole thing had been in the hands of the Great Spirit all along. I told him I had trouble accepting that idea all the way. I found myself leaning toward the thought that a lot of things just kind of fell into place in the way they did. It could have turned out some other way, but it didn't. I guess there's no way to know for sure. I mean, whether it was my fate to become involved, or I just have a stubborn streak and did what I thought I should do, I suppose the end result was the same. Maybe I'll never know.

I opened the throttle a little, and listened to the steady beat of my straight pipes. Good company. I let the miles slip under my tires and drove. I didn't yet know where I'd make my stop when night came. It didn't matter. I knew I'd figure it out when I got there.

~End~

ABOUT THE AUTHOR

Glenn grew up on a farm in the Sierra Nevada foot-hills of California, hiking, hunting, even panning for gold. After college, he served as an officer in the Navy, then earned a doctorate in sociology and taught at a branch of the State University in Connecticut. There, he developed, directed and taught a criminal justice program. Upon retirement, the West drew him back, this time to New Mexico, the setting for his first novel, Murder on Route 66. Currently, Glenn divides his time between living in rural Florida and up-state New York, writing and refurbishing an 1870's-era, creek-side cottage. Whenever possible, he enjoys cooking, riding his own motorcycle and camping.

www.glennnilson.com